LAND OF NO RAIN

LAND OF NO RAIN

AMJAD NASSER

Translated by Jonathan Wright

First published in English in 2014 by
Bloomsbury Qatar Foundation Publishing
Qatar Foundation
PO Box 5825
Doha
Qatar
www.bqfp.com.qa

First published in Arabic in 2011 as *Haythu la tasqut al amtar* by Dar al-Adab

ISBN 9789992194584

Typeset by Hewer Text UK Ltd, Edinburgh
Printed and bound by CPI Group (UK) Ltd, Croydon CR0 4YY

I

Here you are then, going back, the man who changed his name to escape the consequences of what he'd done. It's been a long time since you left, and that was an event that mattered only to the few who took an interest in your case. As usual, those few are constantly declining in number. You're not sure what's left of the flame that burned deep inside you in the days of youth and hope. Your feet have worn out so many pairs of shoes, roaming the streets, walking along dirt paths and paved roads. How many more steps must they take? How much more emotion can your heart muscle handle? What's left that will still excite you? Does the smell of coffee still promise mornings that haven't come? After looking in different directions for so long, will your eyes ever finally converge on the same point? Can you still believe that lie about how cute your cross-eyes are, a lie uttered one day long ago by rosy lips that you were the first to taste? Your eyes are like you. Whenever you look, you have to force them to work together. You were about to ask yourself: on the spiral, or circular, pathway that leads back to the start, who lost and who gained? This question nags you. Another question nags you too, but you've never given it a chance to take shape in your head: did you take the wrong path? It's hard not to ask such questions in a situation such as yours, although you learned in your long

I

exile how to suppress questions you don't like and how to dodge them by procrastination or equivocation. But from now on there can be no more procrastination or equivocation. There was a time when you didn't notice time creeping along the ground and through your body, but now the sound of it is clearly audible.

Everything is endless but nothing remains as it is. That's a lesson your hand has learned, right down to the bones and the nerves; the hand that no longer shakes the air like a fist of bronze, but hovers uncertainly – with bulging veins – over the table, the hand that has to reassess dimensions and sizes, heaviness and lightness. Have you noticed how unsteady it is when you shake hands with people, give directions or touch things? Perhaps not, because against the background noise of flesh and blood, you cannot hear that mysterious and perfidious pickaxe chipping away, as the stones of the fortress start to work loose from the inside. But the rasping noise of that pickaxe comes straight from the lungs. It cannot always be muffled with the palm of a hand or a pocket handkerchief.

Where will you begin your long story, or rather your many stories that overlook each other like the rooms of an old Arab house? You don't know exactly, because the years and events, the faces and voices, are mixed up in your memory. The officers who questioned you at the National Security Agency imposed a sequence of events on you, one that might be better organised from a chronological point of view. But you cannot use the records lying in the drawer assigned to you in that star-shaped stone building. Besides, those cold bureaucratic records are not interested in your inner world, your motives, what lies between the superimposed layers of your self. Those records contain no monologues, no waking dreams, no nightmares, no echoes, no convolutions; only uniformity, a regularity, a linear sequence of events and names. Where among them can you find your mother's soft footsteps at night, as she hovers over the blankets spread on the floor, covering this son or that daughter, opening or closing the windows, rising before anyone else in the morning so that they can wake to the smell of coffee and fresh bread? Where is your father's tall, lean frame, a cigarette hanging from his lip, and his inks, pens and calligraphies that explore the expanses of creation? Where are his leisurely footsteps as he descends the twelve steps to his underground temple? Where are your noisy brothers and kindly sisters? Where is your grandmother's winged shadow, and your grandfather, sitting up straight as a bolt, who stopped writing out those proverbs and sayings when his eyesight started to fade? Where are the faces that somehow imprinted their features on your memory for ever, and the faces whose details have been erased and whose ghostly passage across the screen of your memory keeps you awake at night? Where are the smells that mysteriously preserve the images and feelings you secretly treasure? Where are the pavements, the cold, life when it became just a lucky coincidence, the skies as low as a wall of grey, the long sleepless nights, the cough, the stubborn hopes, the dancing lights of return? There's nothing of all that in those reports, so dry that the paper crinkles, because these are things that don't interest them. These things are useless when the accounts are settled and the harvest is weighed. You didn't answer some of the interrogators' questions, or you responded vaguely and coldly to the questions that no longer interested you. In short, that was the version of the story they wanted, to fill the gaps in their files, not your rambling, tangled story.

So begin here, although it may not be the right beginning, but every story needs to start somewhere.

It came to pass that a plague, reminiscent of an ancient pestilence, swept the City of Red and Grey. You recall the panic that gripped that great conurbation, built of red brick under grey skies. The anarchy. The breakdown in law and order. The great convulsion that affected everything. Because the plague had come almost without warning. Some people attributed it to the large numbers of immigrants, especially those from impoverished countries, and to the crowded slums or asylum camps. Others said the plague was latent in the fabric of the city itself and needed only a catalyst for it to spread. The plague's black wing touched your wife, whom you had met on the Island of the Sun.

You almost perished at the hands of outlaws more than once. Most of your neighbours fled the working-class area where you lived. You don't know what happened to them. The doors of their houses were pulled off their hinges. Some of them were set on fire, some were looted. You found the immigrant grocer who used to sell you goods on credit – although such a practice was unknown in this city – lying in front of his looted shop, his mouth agape as if screaming. So many perished in that unexplained plague, including some of your professional colleagues and some of your drinking companions.

Images of those struck down by the plague – in the streets, in the quarantine centres, at bus stops and on the underground – recur from time to time: of your wife looking at you with weary eyes from behind a glass screen; of the cough that tore the lungs, spitting blood; the almost primitive emotions and behaviour that people exhibited; the face masks that made people look like highwaymen; the X-signs written on walls in thick black ink to distinguish one house from another; the codes used in conversations, none of which you understood; and the weird way that people spoke, as if from the guts and not from the throat.

This memory, or nightmare, recurs time after time. You took backstreets to visit your wife in quarantine in the city centre, which was orderly compared with the suburbs where things had slipped out of control. Three masked men had pounced on you out of the blue. You were carrying a bag with some food in it. They brandished knives and the sharp blades glinted in the tense space between you and them. They told you to put the bag on the ground, that if you wanted to escape with your life you should leave the bag and step aside. You did so. What they found in the bag didn't satisfy the savage eyes behind the masks. They ordered you to give them all the cash you were carrying. You threw your wallet at them from a distance. It seemed there wasn't enough money to make them leave. They saw your wedding ring on your left hand. They gestured to you to take it off. It was hard, not only because you were loath to do so but because your fingers had suddenly swollen. Fear had made your blood flow and your hands were as thick as a couple of fresh peasant loaves. You tried to budge the ring but you couldn't. One of the masked men came forward cautiously. He brandished his knife and you saw the blade. Another man coughed with a sound that seemed to rip his lungs to shreds. It looked like he had to spit. He spat blood on the ground. You could see the colour of his face behind the mask. 'I'm the same colour as you!' you said in the local language to the masked man advancing towards you. That was naive but you couldn't help saying it. 'Shut up! Just shut up!' he barked. He put the tip of the knife between the ring and the flesh and started to lever it. It hurt. You saw drops of blood but you suppressed the pain. The ring didn't come off, so the masked man patiently changed his plan and was about to sever your finger when a police car appeared at the end of the street, saving your finger from amputation.

When you reached the quarantine centre they gave you a tetanus shot and bandaged the wound. Your wife's dull eyes looked at you from behind the glass screen in hope, or despair, or reproach. You couldn't understand how her look could be so changeable, but you will never forget it. You weren't allowed inside the glass enclosure, where dozens of victims lay. You stood outside it. You spoke to her. She couldn't hear you. She seemed to understand what you were saying from your lip movements, because she nodded. Every now and then she had a coughing fit. You couldn't hear it but you could judge its intensity by the way her thin body shook when she turned her head aside. You told her everything would be fine. You weren't sure about that but it's what one has to say in such situations. She moved her head slowly and looked you up and down with her dull eyes until they came to rest on your bandaged hand. You told her it was nothing, just a scratch. Night had fallen. The night held unpleasant surprises in the City of Red and Grey even before the plague spread, let alone after. You always avoided the night. The night, when people fell asleep and talked to themselves on the last buses and trains. The night, when drink brought their dark secrets to the surface and they vented the anger that was hidden behind their daytime masks – the masks that made them appear so composed to those who could be taken in – or jabbered in strange languages that sounded barbaric to ears that did not know what they were talking about.

The masked staff at the quarantine centre kept you in the hallway. There were others like you who had nowhere else to go. In the morning you crept out. The newborn day was a dome of grey. The city centre, usually crowded with pedestrians at all times of day and night, was almost empty. Few shops had opened their doors. Guards stood in front of them on the alert. The cafés where youngsters would drink coffee, smoke and shout at each other in high spirits were mostly closed. Mannequins gazed out from the shop windows like frozen idols, displaying the fashions of a hypothetical summer. The air was so thick you could touch it. The tall trees crouched like mythical creatures about to pounce. In the street the manholes that led underground were uncovered, and foul odours emerged from them. Soldiers armed with strange devices stood guard in front of sensitive government facilities. Intermittently and cautiously, spectres crossed from one pavement to the other. Police cars and ambulances ploughed through streets that were almost empty of cars, the sound of their tyres amplified in the muteness of the morning.

There had been a time when faces from all corners of the world had cut a path along the city's narrow pavements and down the underground tunnels, when young men and women had embraced with a physical freedom that was sometimes embarrassing, when buskers had played music, sometimes cheerful and sometimes sad, in front of the big shops and at the entrances to the gloomy netherworld, in this grey-skied Babel crowned with the gold of the colonial era. It never occurred to you, even in your worst nightmares, that this city would descend into ruin and see the reappearance of primitive weapons, obsolete symbols and emotions you thought you had left behind in your long journey.

In the great square and the cobbled streets that radiated out from it in all directions, the desolation reminded you of an old film of the area, deserted after some disaster you don't recall. But you do remember the hero of the film running through the empty streets, crossing the bridge with the two stone towers, entering one building and emerging from another, being ambushed by a wild gang, getting away and being on the run throughout the film. It's as if the film was a terrible warning, except that in reality, but not in the film, people were moving about – some wearing masks on their faces and gloves on their hands, covering anything that would give away their colour, their features or their identity. Masked against the raging storm of fear and danger. Was it similar to what happened in the City of Siege and War? No. Maybe. You don't know, because your nightmares have merged with reality. Your ability to judge has diminished. You can no longer be sure. Time has dissolved, and the events and the faces have merged together.

So you've returned. It's been twenty years since you fled Hamiya. Of course, you don't need anyone to remind you how many years it's been, but you believe, as you put it during casual conversation on the balcony of your family's house, between coughing fits, that time has unexpectedly played a cruel trick on you – how is it that things that should have disappeared have survived, while many faces have lost their details? That's just a roundabout way of talking about time, because instead of saying *time*, you said *things* and *faces*. But the name doesn't change anything, because time, as you know (do you really know?), does not defer to hopes, however fervent they might be, nor to resolutions, even if they are as firm as steel. Time has its own ways, direct or cunning, of achieving its purposes, and it never fails to hit the mark. No glancing blows, or blows outside the line. Time is also a train that does not prefer any particular station, even if it lingers here or hastens there. Maybe you can't hear its whistle till it's left, but its effects are visible on faces, on hands, in the way people stand and in the pictures hanging on the walls. The people who waited for you saw the whole map of your long journey on your face. Twenty years is not a number. In fact, in a case such as yours, it might be a life that has run its course. But do you know what's good about it? That the days roll on, impervious, for everyone. They hone, erode and level everything they touch. Even your double, the person you used to be, the one who was frozen in his twenties by some mysterious disease, knows what that means.

Once upon a time you were considered a hero, or a conspirator. A brave young man who either – in the eyes of some abroad – took part in a heroic act, or whose head – in the eyes of others here – had been poisoned by imported ideas and who was implicated in a reckless act. You and your double, the man you used to be, both paid the price for what you did. While he survived as a ghost or a freak, growing no older and no younger, preserving a name and a life that had been nipped in the bud, you had to tramp the pavements and face the cold – battered by winds that blew your tattered sail far away. Now that matters have changed, the names and the acts balance out on the scales of insubstantial oblivion. You're no longer a hero or a conspirator. Just an old man, half forgotten, coming back after twenty years of struggle, pursuing ideas that did not bring about much change in your country, and perhaps nowhere else either. Your double, the person you used to be, was tough on you. He seemed to have been waiting for this chance for a long time. In his head he had a long list of simmering questions. He cornered you. He crossed his arms over his chest, in the same old boyish way, and stood in front of you like a stubborn inquisitor. Apparently the interrogation you underwent at the National Security Agency wasn't enough for him, even if the sentence against you had lapsed because of a general amnesty that included even those who had been given tougher sentences. When you arrived at the airport they let you leave with your relatives. They knew what had happened, of course, and they showed understanding for your situation, but they asked you to 'drop in' on them when you were ready. Your friend Salem, the former National Security officer, from the half of his memory that is still functioning, told you that in the NSA they never destroy a file, however old it is or however many officials come and go. 'Because the NSA is a memory that never grows old or forgets,' he said, like someone mouthing a text he has learnt by heart. You went to the star-shaped headquarters, that stone building you know so well, which from a distance used to look like a spaceship just landed from another planet. You were surprised at the change in the surroundings, where no one used to venture and where even birds dared not fly overhead. Now there were carts selling food, people authenticating documents, vendors selling cold drinks, petitioners and people who wrote official letters for a living, people of different ages, variously dressed, all stationed in front of the NSA building. You underwent the interrogation, twenty years late. They didn't call it an interrogation; they just said, 'Come and have a cup of coffee with us.' You were not tetchy, as you often are. You were cold, even remote – I might almost say prudent – as though it were all about someone other than you. There was nothing new that you could add to the thick files piled in front of the three young, nameless officers, who were dressed in almost identical civilian clothes. You laughed when you saw the small pile. You were about to have a coughing fit. The officer who seemed to have the highest rank asked, 'Why do you laugh?' 'Have I committed all that?' you asked, pointing at the files heaped on the table. You knew that trick. You'd come across it in the Organisation, in psychological training to handle interrogation. It's to make you feel they know every single detail about you and your doings. It's here in these files, you can't deny it! You thought to yourself, 'It looks like these guys have preserved something of the traditions of the past.' But still, you knew they had plenty on you. Your disguise had not misled them for long. They found you out shortly after you took refuge in the City Overlooking the Sea. They had eyes and ears there. That didn't surprise you. You know the NSA was active in that city, which was a playground for numerous similar agencies. It may even have been the most active. There were also suspicions that there were infiltrators, despite the filters that new recruits had to pass through before they acquired membership of the Organisation. Penetration is to be expected in clandestine work. It can't be avoided entirely. Political activists in Hamiya knew that when it came to bugging, surveillance, interrogation, propaganda and psychological warfare techniques the NSA was more advanced than its counterparts in neighbouring countries. Inside the star-shaped stone building, a place with almost no windows or balconies, perched alone on the edge of the wasteland, there were specialists in psychology, in reading between the lines, in propagating rumours and exposing disguises. The NSA had interrogators who did not use traditional methods for extracting confessions and information from political activists. They relied on cunning modern techniques they had acquired abroad. Penetration was inevitable, but the NSA spread rumours that exaggerated the extent of it, in order to keep the opposition forces off balance and make them have doubts about themselves.

Some people suspected that your friend Mahmoud had been a plant. You hadn't suspected him. You knew how he tended to seek the limelight, to stand out and compete. But you didn't suspect him. You defended him as much as you could. You offered arguments and evidence in his favour, such as the fact that Mahmoud knew about the poultry farm where you were hiding before you escaped abroad. If he had been a plant he would have given you away. Those who suspected Mahmoud told you this wasn't proof. It could have been the opposite – to give you that impression, while he went on working for them abroad. You remembered that argument about Mahmoud at one of the coffee sessions in the NSA, when the interrogators referred to the apartment that you'd lived in briefly, in the City Overlooking the Sea, and the weapons that were in it and the maps for the operation in which they stormed the Hamiyan embassy in some Asian capital. They described the apartment in detail and its location in the maze of lanes, which floor it was on, what the door handle was made of, the number of rooms, and the colour of the curtains. You remembered the man in charge of 'external operations' in the Organisation, who had put you up in that apartment. You had a fleeting memory of meeting him in a local coffee shop. You remembered his white face with sharp features and blondish hair, but when he laughed, for whatever reason you don't now recall, you could see his decaying teeth. While one of the young interrogators was talking about the apartment, you were thinking about how the external operations boss had always avoided laughing, in fact had almost refrained from smiling, probably because of his teeth. You thought to yourself that he must have had a complex about them. You have your own complex – you have a slight squint in your left eye, so you can't look straight at the person you're talking to. You've devised a studied turn of the head, so that both your eyes are directed at the person. You've tested the manoeuvre dozens of times in front of the mirror until you've mastered it. Your feelings about your cross-eyes only changed when the woman you loved said how fetching they were. Except for Mahmoud, you don't remember anyone visiting you in the temporary apartment. Oh yes, you do. There was that girl you met in some bar in the city. Mahmoud was with you too. You don't know how you ended up walking into that bar. You wanted a drink and you went into more than one bar in an area that was almost deserted because of the war. You had a drink here and a drink there. In that dimly lit bar, which reminded both of you of one you used to frequent in Hamiya, you found some girls smoking sullenly at the wooden counter, as dark as the bar itself. You don't remember how many there were, four or five. There were two down-at-heel men drinking and smoking, pensively, as though in another world. When you went into the bar – you were two tall young men, one with long hair and a droopy moustache, the other with short hair and a trimmed moustache – a tremor ran through the dark-skinned girls. You ordered beer. You wanted to round off your bar crawl, the first you'd had in this city, with a cold beer. You sat at a wooden table with long benches along either side, rather like a school desk. Two women came up flirtatiously and asked to join you for a drink. You didn't object. The one sitting next to you was older than you. In her thirties, you guessed. She could tell from your strong accent that you were a foreigner. She asked you where you were from, and you told her. That was your first mistake, or rather the second, because for security reasons your instructions were to avoid dubious contacts such as these. Out of drunkenness or desire, or both, you took her back to that apartment and slept with her. You're almost smiling to yourself now as you remember how clever she was at pretending to be aroused and enjoying it, which was convincing at the time. You gave her some money and she left. That was your third mistake. Was it her? You thought about it, but no. She hadn't sought you out. It was you who'd staggered into that dark bar. You're no longer interested in who the informer was. You had nothing to do with the embassy-storming operation. For a start you weren't close to the external operations department. It's true that, like others, you underwent military training, but you didn't work in the military wing. Your work in the Organisation was in the public relations and mobilisation department. When the external operations boss put you up in that apartment, it was at least a year after the embassy operation and its aftermath. The aim of the operation was apparently not to kill anyone but only to hold the ambassador hostage and exchange him for some prisoners from the Organisation. No one knows exactly who opened fire first: the ambassador's bodyguards or one of the gunmen. Whoever had fired the first shot, the operation ended in a bloodbath. The ambassador, two of his bodyguards and three of the gunmen were killed. The support team was arrested but they did not stay long in prison because the external operations department of the Organisation, in collusion with a friendly country, abducted the ambassador of the Asian country in the capital of that country, and he was exchanged for the support team. You told them you had nothing to do with the operation, and the one who seemed to have the highest rank said they knew that, but they wanted to hear your version of it. He also said it was a procedural matter because all the sentences had been dropped. It was just a matter of closing the files! You told him that the external operations chief in the Organisation had disappeared while crossing the border of a state sympathetic towards you, and there was no trace of him. In the tone of someone who knows everything, he said they knew that and it had happened ten years ago. All you could do was ask him, with a trace of sarcasm, why he didn't ask the secretary-general of the Organisation, who had returned to the country before you. The officer who seemed to be the most senior of the three concurred. 'We've already asked him,' he said, in the same sarcastic tone. 'In fact we've asked all your comrades who've returned.'

I am Younis al-Khattat, and the man who has returned is me twenty years ago. I'd been waiting for ages for the opportunity that arose that night when we got talking, on the balcony of our house, amid bouts of coughing and sweating that made me feel sorry for him, though I suppressed my sympathy. I didn't tell him a story as he'd expected. I spoke after he'd finished telling his own story, about the other man who had the same name as him and who practised the same profession. He wanted that story to be a metaphor for, or a counterpart to, my story about him. But he chose the wrong beginning with that story, which struck me as a little feeble, the way he invented someone who happened to share his pseudonym and of whose existence he wasn't previously aware. Besides, knowing that the other guy existed didn't change the course of his life. It was just a random coincidence of the kind that keeps happening to people without becoming a pattern or amounting to anything of consequence. I told him that his story was not enough to say that things were quits. I made fun of the poems in which he mourned his father and mother, and those in which he alluded to Roula. I said, 'Which pavement were you hanging around on when your father was found dead in his studio, with a cigarette butt in the left corner of his mouth? In which bar or café were you boozing or sipping a cup of coffee while the cancer ate away at your mother in Hamiya's public hospital?' I also said that no words, however remorseful or apologetic, could make up for the way his mother had gazed westward, the direction she thought had swallowed him up for ever. I also told him that Roula had not betrayed him and Khalaf had not deceived him. I reminded him of Muhsin's suicide. I told him that comrade Hanan had died, that Hala had married a businessman and Hasib had disappeared. I told him that Tom Thumb was the head of a smuggling gang and that Salman, his first poetry teacher, had become an evangelical preacher who toured the country towns and villages. I mentioned names that surprised him and others that he remembered straight away. I showed him a toughness that he wasn't expecting. I played devil's advocate with him. He had to hear a voice other than the voices of his brothers and sisters saying how much they had missed him, although they had coped in his absence. Their reminiscences and hearty laughs were all genuine but it's also true that life here had moved on, detached from him, without the need for his existence, because life doesn't wait for anyone and it doesn't stop when one person gets off. This is a simple fact known to the ignorant and the learned alike. I'm amazed how it escaped him. Roula waited as long as she could. Men were courting her, men who wanted a wife or companion, but she kept turning them down. She offered many excuses and reasons, some of which were convincing and others less so. Khalaf stood by her throughout. He did not hide his relationship with his fugitive friend. He did not dissociate himself from him, although that was not easy for a security man in Hamiya.

He has to know the truth and no one is better placed than me to tell him. If a drop of my blood still runs in his veins he'll know I'm the only person who didn't lie to him or humour him, because how can one lie to oneself? Of course, there are people who do, people who deceive themselves, but I think that one decisive moment face to face with one's self is enough to show one the truth. There are others who didn't lie to him either: Salem, for example, at least when the conscious half of his brain was able to receive the right signal and he knew who was speaking to him. Wahid brought back memories of a bunch of youthful pranks. And his brother Shihab is rude enough to tell him things he might not like. He believes Shihab. If he wasn't so rude, Shihab would be a copy of his father.

He looked into a mirror and asked me if he had changed much. I said, 'Of course you've changed. Everyone changes,

17

what else do you expect?' But out of compassion I did not tell him that the people who were waiting for him at the airport did not recognise him at first. All his family were there, except his late father, his mother and his elder brother, who lives in the Land of Palm Trees and Oil. And when he came through customs pushing his trolley with his suitcase and some plastic bags he almost passed them by without them recognising him. They didn't believe he was the same person who had once been as tall and elegant as a rattan cane. The torch of the movement. The one on whose shoulders all the world's devils liked to play. Cheerful. Noisy. Cruel and compassionate. It's true they had seen his picture in magazines and newspapers, but pictures are one thing and reality is something else. With their expectant eyes they saw what the hammers of time had wrought on his face, his shoulders, his frame and the movement of his hands. They heard his cough, which he tried to cover with a pocket handkerchief that he carried in his hand. His languor was evident, and his helplessness looked deeply ingrained. But members of his family told him he looked younger and healthier than he did in the pictures. It wasn't true. What mattered to them was that he had returned, not how or in what shape. They colluded, without any overt agreement, in ignoring anything that might spoil the pleasure of his happy return, while for him it was hard enough coming to terms with the shock. Their collusion worked, for a while. He went along with it readily. The City of Red and Grey came to his mind by way of comparison between here and there, in terms of behaviour, orderliness and development, and strangely the comparison usually ended in favour of the last place on his long journey – the City of Red and Grey that he had just left, with his frame bowed and his pocket handkerchief covered in red stains.

That was in the daytime, surrounded by listeners with the intense curiosity of provincials. At night it was a different matter. The whole night was his, the night when his cough and his insomnia never failed to start on time, along with the random disconnected images that crossed his mind. No one can stop the machine of memory from working. Nothing has been invented, as far as he knows, that can tame memory, make it work on demand. Even I, with my few exaggerated memories, cannot fend off attacks by the most unpleasant of them.

One afternoon his brother Shihab took them for a drive in his father's old Land Rover, which for years they had used for hunting trips. He thought it a good omen that the vehicle, which he used to call the mechanical steed, was still in use, but he was surprised to find that the civilian airport, which used to be on the outskirts of the city, was now part of the suburbs. He looked out of the car window at the passing scenes but found no reference in his memory: the mansions, the tourist resorts, the big malls, the temporary encampments of people displaced by the blood and fire sweeping the country next door, the vast advertising hoardings for five or six mobile phone companies – written with outrageous spelling mistakes – the glass towers crowned by enormous dishes, the children and old people offering seasonal fruit and vegetables from plastic crates, the shanty towns built of corrugated iron and cardboard, teeming with children and the unemployed. He was filled with a kind of aesthetic numbness at such eyesores and at the renowned establishments that had made the fields of wheat and corn, the groves of pine and juniper trees, a distant memory. He recalled a famous local song that spoke of how the country girls walked around carrying water jars on their heads in the afternoon. He told himself that even the songs failed the test: it was hard to listen to them now that the things they described had changed. He was surprised when the car skidded on the edge of a roundabout in the centre of which stood a large statue of Hamiya's eagle. The venerable bird looked old, scarcely able to spread the vast wings that used to cast their fearsome shadow over the country. The only familiar landmark that the car passed was this old statue. He suspected his memory was at fault. His brother Shihab smoked throughout the journey, leaving his returning brother to see and compare in silence the new reality with the images he remembered. He asked Shihab if all these buildings had existed before. Shihab told him that most of them were new and that the ring road meant that people going in this direction were spared the trouble of driving through the downtown area, which was congested with cars and pedestrians. But as soon as the Land Rover started to emerge from the built-up labyrinth around the airport, with its chaos and its shabbiness, the space opened out in front of them. The endless desert showed its yellow face and he managed to catch blurred glimpses of shepherds, wrapped as usual in their heavy cloaks.

II

Once you were a poet. Apparently you no longer know what poetry is or how it's written. Now you write articles and biographies, without parting company with poetry's uncertain, hesitant attitude towards the world. Some of what you write is personal, and some of it public, though it's hard for you to differentiate between the two. You don't categorise what you write. You just write, but you believe that, besides biographies, you are writing poetical articles. This is not a category that's recognised on the literary scene, and it's hard to persuade people that it exists, so you don't speak about it openly. The truth is you don't care what it's called. In the prime of your youth you cared. You and others fought battles over form and content and the link between poetry, reality and the reader. But you no longer do that, now that you harbour doubts. Now you believe that categorising and pigeon-holing don't achieve anything. That they're just labels. Your problem is that whenever you write something you rush it into print, especially when you're working on newspapers and magazines, which, for those who don't know, are machines that never stop turning, churning out thin gruel and rich cream in equal measure. You're hasty. Haste is a trait that's ingrained in you. Despite all your attempts to take it easy and slow down, you can't change. You see it as a genetic defect that you have to live with. You write in a hurry. You publish what you write without any prior plan or any clear concept or vision of where your writing is leading. But when you reread everything you have written, one piece after another, you can see a common thread, or a mysterious pointer, always pointing in the same direction, even though the pieces were written at different times and under the sway of different emotions. Only then do you get a sense of that obscure something that drives you on towards the lights that flicker in the distance. Then you regret rushing into print, not rushing into writing, and you say to yourself, 'If only I had sat on what I wrote before publishing it.' (Despite your long waiting in exile, patience is your deadly enemy.) Perhaps that way you could have come up with a work that had organic unity, or a harmonious sequence in which one part led to the rest, without interruptions, gaps or jumps. But no way! Only after it was too late did that kind of prudence or farsightedness descend on you from the ethereal heights. But that's all in the past and nothing can be done about it. Now the situation is different.

Behind a window overlooking the street, as you watch a bird tracking prey you cannot see, you've started to write your last book. The book of all your books. You've decided to take a different approach this time. Because this time is different: there's no newspaper or magazine waiting for you to throw it a piece of your flesh (an extreme metaphor for words, which you often used without realising what it meant; you just liked the sound of it). You've decided to set your writing free from the dates, parenthetical clauses, digressions and proper names that usually weigh it down. For a long time you saw the latter as essential props, before you discovered that their solidity was deceptive. You've resolved to ignore them or replace them with description. You have a rationale in your head for this plan: you want to free yourself from them. But you're not sure about the validity of this reason, because it's hard to free oneself from names. It's also hard to free oneself of chronic habits, favourite words and obsessive ideas.

Apparently things don't disappear completely. They don't vanish for ever. It's like the scientific principle I once read about in class, that matter doesn't disappear, it just changes from one state to another.

You're a man familiar with life under the roof of matrimony, a roof that rests on the twin pillars of patience and promises.

Remember that.

The boat on which you left the City of Siege and War sailed to the Island of the Sun. There you met a young sociologist who had rebelled against her family and, like you, had fallen under the spell of ideas about replacing the corrupt old world with a new world where everyone would be equal. That's the echo of an old way of speaking, which many people today consider to be intellectual naivety, even though its red banners once fluttered on the skyline. The Island of the Sun teemed with refugees, people fleeing the City of Siege and War. On that island, its humped form like that of a giant tropical tortoise, there were political activists, guerrilla fighters and arms dealers, diplomats and spies, poets and writers, artists, newspaper and magazine editors and printers, wanderers, adventurers, profiteers and purveyors of lies, cooks and pros-titutes, musicians and singers – a vast throng tossed there by the cycle of successive wars that raged. Then came the thou-sand-day siege and the occupation. You met her at a seminar on the lessons to be drawn from what was happening in the City of Siege and War. She was talking about the double standard that intellectuals apply towards women – how they speak about them in the world at large and how they treat them at home. They ask women to liberate themselves and rebel, but they keep a close eye on their wives, sisters and daughters. What she said was strong and measured, without emotion or histrionics, despite her tremulous tone.

You liked what she said; in fact you liked her. You met several times. You were famous, to some extent, within a narrow clique of intellectuals – a poet and activist from a country ruled by a military dynasty of men with ginger hair. So it wasn't hard to introduce yourself. At first you were surprised that a young woman from a country so isolated from its surroundings would rebel and throw herself into public affairs, would run away and cross borders, through dusty towns, along dry riverbeds, to settle in a city that was vulnerable to wars and sieges. She was rather pretty, attractive in fact. She didn't wear make-up and rarely used perfume. That made her more attractive in your view, along of course with the intelligence that shone in her eyes. After two or three meetings you knew part of her story. She had been married, briefly, to a young revolutionary from her own country. They had met while studying in the City of Red and Grey and fallen in love. In their case love and ideology went hand in hand. In their meetings, far from the eyes of family and the traditions of their country, ideas and books were just as present as emotions and sex. That was rare among the young people of their country, which had been indoctrinated by a strict religious sect. They married. But the marriage did not last long, because the young revolutionary quickly changed. Her differentness, which he had liked abroad, began to trouble him back at home. Then it began to annoy him. Then it started to keep him awake at night: her smoking, the way she crossed her legs on an evening out or at a family gathering, her lack of interest in dressing up, the way she was so candid with her opinions, the way she objected to any word or deed she didn't like, the clarity of her ideas and her conduct, her interest in public affairs. In short, her attempt to pursue what they believed in and what they had done abroad, and her uncompromising attitude towards the conventions of their country. The marriage ended in a divorce that no one favoured, even those closest to her. She was on assignment when she came to the City of Siege and War for the first time. It amazed her that there should be a city in the region that was so open-minded, so pluralistic, with such a lively social life despite the occasional outbreaks of gunfire. She said this was the city where she dreamed of living, and she came again to settle, running away to join the forces of the revolution, which put up posters of its martyrs and leaders on the approaches to the city, with slogans promising a new world.

It wasn't long into your relationship with her that you got married. After that you lived in as much harmony as is possible for two bodies, two spirits from two different backgrounds under a single roof. You were living your present, that moment when you met her. This is true. You never thought about the fact that you were not the first man in her life, because she too was not the first woman in your life. What mattered to you was that you should have nothing in common with that young revolutionary who had sold out as soon as he went back to his country. You would analyse with her the contradiction between the principles and behaviour displayed by the revolutionaries in our region. As though reciting from a sacred text, you attributed this to the fact that objective circumstances were not yet ripe and that ingrained traditions vigorously resisted new ideas. But this was only what you said at the start of your relationship, before you got married. You liked that. You praised what she said without reservation. You endorsed her arguments and her conclusions about the double standards of intellectuals. In fact you would even go a step further. You seemed to be in complete agreement on these matters. After living under the same roof you changed somewhat. You changed gradually. You no longer wanted to take part in these discussions. On such issues you were terser, less enthusiastic, less effusive than before. She was more lucid than you, and she remained so. It was you who still preserved inside you areas shrouded in darkness that, with the passage of time, you surrounded with barbed wire.

In your final years in the City of Red and Grey, you had the impression that she had the upper hand in the household. It was an impression rooted in traditional attitudes that you hadn't completely shaken off, but it was not necessarily the reality of the situation. Having studied sociology in that same city, she had found a good full-time job in an organisation that dealt with immigrants. You had a sporadic income. You helped set up a magazine – along with others who had escaped from your part of the world with their writing skills and their ideas (and with their skins) – as a platform for freedom, to expose the corruption and despotism of the forces in control there, but you left the magazine after it was co-opted. With their vast amounts of money or their pistols with silencers, those forces penetrated countries of refuge and asylum to bring to heel those who had strayed from the flock, those who had fled the hell at home. Some gave in under the pressure of making ends meet, while others said with derision, 'If that's how it is, why don't we work with the very source instead of with its agents?' That magazine was almost the last of the publications to join the choir in which the fugitives from hell raggedly sang the infernal national anthem, turning sour milk, as the proverb goes, into cottage cheese. Needless to say, you stopped working at the magazine and started to write here and there, leaving one failed project in order to embark on another. Which made you even more reclusive.

When she was going over, for some reason, some of her old stories about her young revolutionary husband, she would ask you whether the subject bothered you. With just one or two words or a shake of the head you would say no. She didn't like that. She thought it showed that you weren't interested in her, not that you believed that her right to her own past was non-negotiable and required no apologies. Because there was nothing she needed to be embarrassed about or apologise for. Her suggestion that you weren't interested would annoy you. But was it without basis? Did it occur to you to analyse the components of your alleged position? It didn't. You seemed to be afraid to go deeper into the subject, in case you might be included among those comrades that the great revolutionary once likened to radishes – red only on the outside.

Your marriage wasn't bad. You didn't completely fail to live up to the adjustments, concessions and promises required when two people live under the same roof, but nonetheless you sometimes felt, or dreamt, that you were still the adolescent you once were. You saw yourself as a young man with long hair and a droopy moustache, running through the stations on a radio that would fit in the palm of your hand, in search of those heart-rending songs that were popular in the prime of your youth. That feeling, or dream, did not last long: your wife's voice, reminding you that this or that needed doing, brought you back to the fact that you were with her, to the conjugal bond and its obligations. And then you're a solid man. That's how you appear to those who see you, or how you would like others to see you. Beauty unsettles you. You get excited. You cry. But that doesn't last long either. You don't have any obvious tendency to become addicted to anything. And you thought your wife had no doubts about you, was in fact immune to narrow feelings of jealousy, until a certain piece of paper crossed your path.

A colleague of your wife's and the colleague's husband, local people, had invited you to spend the weekend with them in a town in the south where they had a country house. You had visited the town and the area several times. It was famous for its old castle, which reminded you of similar castles in the world you came from, and it was warmer than the City of Red and Grey. You used to go there 'to free inspiration from its bottle', as you put it. It was an offhand rhetorical phrase, but of your own making. You would sit on a wooden bench by a small river with sheep bleating on the banks, their tails like dogs' tails, not like the famous fat-tailed sheep of your country. You would sit there like a fisherman waiting for a bite, with the big castle in front of you and the little rippling river running by your side. You did write, but as for 'freeing inspiration from its bottle', that's a different matter.

You and your wife took the train, through long dark tunnels and across deep green pastures where you saw cows with their heads to the ground, heavy louring clouds, and horses wrapped in blankets like mules. The people in that country don't meet their guests at stations or airports, as they do in your country. Your wife's colleague didn't live far from the station: a fifteen-minute walk or less. You walked down a long street lined with identical terraced houses with red tiled roofs and marked with numbers. Your wife suddenly bent down and picked up a piece of paper from the ground. You don't know what made her do that, because she didn't usually stare at the ground, as you have long been in the habit of doing, looking for things that have fallen from people's pockets. It must have been your bad luck that made her pick up this piece of paper, or maybe something else. The piece of paper was old. That was obvious from its appearance – the creases and the lined paper. You saw your wife shiver silently after opening it up and reading some lines. When she looked at you out of the corner of her eye, you realised it had something to do with you. 'What's up?' you asked. She didn't say anything. She thrust the piece of paper at you. The handwriting was similar to your own, which unconsciously imitates a hand you knew well. It was a love letter but you had no idea where or when it was written. The handwriting was very like yours, and your wife knew the name of the woman to whom it was addressed and something of what had happened between you and her. It was an old affair, from the distant past. Nonetheless you had always tried to avoid talking about it with your wife, not because she was jealous of a woman who now had another life far away, but maybe because of your reserved nature, even though you could be talkative when you were interested and in a good mood.

You can control when you speak out and when you hold your tongue, but how can you control what you say in your sleep? In the dreams and nightmares you have. Those long rambling monologues that your wife sometimes wakes up to, and then she strokes your head so tenderly.

How could it have happened?

The letter quoted a short poem in traditional metre from your book *Tilka allati,* or *That Which*, and the poem included clear references to your first love. In those days you hadn't yet had a book published in Hamiya, and *Tilka allati* didn't contain a single poem in traditional metre. And after you fled your country you gave up writing in traditional metre because the jaunty rhythms and the artificial diction made you sick. In prose and narrative you began to discover latent poetical possibilities and a freedom of expression that were hard to find in poems of a genre dominated by big issues, poems full of slogans, polemics and angry ranting.

Although your wife maintained her composure she wasn't convinced by your arguments or by the evidence you started to lay out: first, the fact that there was no signature on the letter; second, that names and even handwriting can be alike; and third, that *Tilka allati* didn't contain any poems in traditional metre. Finally, after you ran out of arguments, you said, 'Even if we suppose the poem is mine, that's not evidence that I wrote the letter. People have a right to quote a poem, even one by an obscure poet.'

Without telling you, your wife seemed to think that your first love might also have moved to your last country of exile. You knew your hunch was on the right track because married couples, after living together for a while, can read their partners' thoughts even as they take shape in their minds. Your brother Shihab had also called to tell you about rumours that a general amnesty for convicted fugitives was imminent (such rumours came and went and then reappeared without anyone knowing who started them or how true they were). Before ending the call he had told you that your wife had called him to ask how they were and that among other things she had asked about Roula, your first love. Your wife was dumbfounded when she found out that Roula had never left your country and that in that hot and arid place she had three or four children. Although the weekend in that country town passed well enough, afterwards you noticed that the papers piled on the table in your study were not as tidy as they had been, your pockets had been turned out, and your wife was all ears whenever you spoke with anyone on the phone, especially in your native language.

One can't be unlucky all the time.
That would be against the nature of things.
That person they call Sharara,
The epitome of pessimism and bad luck,
Even he strikes lucky some of the time.

You and your wife were listening to a serious radio station. You rarely watched television, because the obtrusive pictures left no room for imagination. There was a programme on about how the things we lose or throw away, such as papers, books, watches and pens, can come back to haunt us. The subject of the programme hit a sore spot, as they say. It frightened you. You tried to change the station. You were worried its revelations might corroborate the evidence against you. But your wife, who knew intuitively what was going on in your head, insisted on listening to the end. The presenter was interviewing a middle-aged woman. You gathered this from her voice and from the events that came up in the programme.

Judging by the rustling that you heard, similar to the sound of someone handling papers, the interviewer seemed to be showing her something. 'Is this your handwriting?' he asked her. It took some time before the woman said, 'Yes, it's my handwriting.' The interviewer said, 'I'm showing you some pages, just at random, but can you remember when and where you wrote them?'

There was another silence. Then the woman spoke, with something like a sigh. 'My God, it's a long time ago. I don't know how long.' You found out that the pages he had shown her had been torn out of a diary she had written during an affair with a resistance leader in a city the name of which you didn't catch. The city was besieged and then occupied, when the woman was a student in her twenties. She was in love with the field commander in the city. When the city fell under occupation, she didn't leave the city, unlike some of the other foreign students there, but stayed alongside the resistance fighter. But the emotions that arise in such circumstances apparently do not remain unchanged. The occupation forces were driven out of the city and the field commander became prominent in society, famous for his heroic exploits. The young woman went back to her country to arrange to move back and live with him, but the former commander sent her a letter telling her that he was now having a relationship with another woman. 'Sorry, our relationship was more a matter of humanitarian and political solidarity than of love.' That's what he wrote. The effect of the letter was devastating. She didn't know what to do. Her first reaction was to throw her diary, in which she had recorded private and public moments related to the field commander and the resistance, into the waste-paper basket.

You didn't learn anything about the young woman's anguish, because she didn't speak of it. It seemed that little of her pain remained, so long after the wound. But you did find out how the memory came back to her. The diary had been found by the programme producers, who would retrieve people's lost or forgotten moments. That was the special feature of this radio programme, which was popular among men and women with little to celebrate or regret. Time generally ensures that such feelings fade away.

In the flea markets common in that country, shoppers such as you can find personal possessions such as underwear, pictures, diaries and medals from the world wars: amazing things. Amazing to you at least, for whom such possessions are personal and intimate and should not end up being desecrated in that way. It was in such a market that the producers had come across the woman's diary. As for how the diary, thrown in the rubbish in a moment of anger, had reached the flea market, that's another story, but it shows that what for us is a final act might be the beginning for someone else, and that our decisions about the fate of something do not necessarily come to pass. It seems that everything has another life even when it's thrown in the rubbish bin. Anyway, what matters is that the producers had tracked down the woman through the address written on the inside cover of the diary. That detail didn't surprise you because you know that people in that country can be born and die, generation after generation, in a house with the same address, in a neighbourhood where the long streets lined with houses do not change. Even the trees are not uprooted or replaced unless a storm blows them down or they are attacked by deadly insects, some of which, they say, arrive on immigrant ships.

At the end of the programme the presenter asked the woman, 'What are you going to do with the diary?'

The woman paused for a while, and then said, 'I don't know. I might read it, or I might throw it straight in the bin.' She seemed to regret giving a hasty answer that might suggest resentment unworthy of her pride. Of course it wasn't possible to see her face, but that moment of silence on the radio weighed heavily. The woman, her old wound exposed to an inquisitive audience, quickly laughed – a jerky laugh – then added with a tongue-in-cheek warning, 'As long as you don't bring it back to me again!'

The story had the effect of magic.

III

You don't believe in signals the way your father did. You waited nonetheless. You wouldn't just wait, you would cross your arms and wait, or lay your right hand casually on the table in a café where you were the only customer. That wasn't exactly how you waited. You have lived and worked in several countries and moved around. In the meantime the blood in your veins has run fast and slow. You have fingered the secret cross on your stomach thousands of times. You have gasped and sighed endlessly. You have tasted a hundred flavours of coffee. You have smoked countless cigarettes and drunk enough to wreck a camel's liver. Faces that you don't remember have passed you by, and others have stamped their cheerfulness or their melancholy on your memory for ever. You have slept in many beds, some for a single night. You have smelled the scents of women – some more than once, others never to be smelled again. Suns have set and suns have risen. You have looked up at skies with big stars that lit up your sleepless nights, sometimes at skies where no stars shone and no meteorites fell. You have walked with many people (though fewer and fewer) along roads with landmarks that grew indistinct or disappeared entirely when you reached them. The idea of going back dogged you at every step, like your shadow. It didn't happen when you wanted, but much later. The shadow faded and kept its distance, but it never completely abandoned you.

Some beginnings are acute angles, and others obtuse.
A decisive beginning puts footsteps on roads that may be
    long or may be short,
And this probably happens early.
There are abortive beginnings, appointments awaited,
Circuitous routes, twisting and turning,
This is a foregone conclusion.

From time to time you would go to the flea market in the City of Red and Grey. In that city, which had taken in many such as you, you spent a part of your sojourn, your exile, your wanderings, call it what you will, waiting for the signal to return. You used to visit flea markets in your own country. You continued to do so anywhere your footsteps led you. In the City of Red and Grey these markets are usually held on Saturdays and Sundays. People there sell some of their possessions, because they're bored with them or they need the money, or they might deal in antiques, local and foreign. Such markets are common in today's world, which is afflicted with a modern scourge, unknown to people in the past, called consumerism. You don't always go to these markets with the intention to buy, but you might need things that aren't available in ordinary markets, so you resort to these markets that are set up haphazardly in public spaces, empty playgrounds, in schoolyards or outside churches. The main reason why you go to these markets is curiosity, the secret desire to find out what people possess and what they are getting rid of, as if you were looking inside houses that it's not easy for foreigners like you to enter. The people of the City of Red and Grey have no scruples about selling things they no longer need, even their underwear. How often have you seen pretty girls at wooden stalls offering their tiny coloured panties, some of them mere thongs, or bras of various cup sizes? How often have you seen letters written during one of the world wars, tied together with silk thread, or black-and-white photographs of men and women with movie-star haircuts and in fashions from the 1940s and 1950s, offered for sale by old women? That's your explanation of why you go to those markets. But some might say it's blatant nostalgia for similar markets, with goods less varied or daring, that you knew in your own country.

In such markets in Hamiya the brand names – some famous and some unknown – would whisk you away to distant lands without you needing to move an inch. The people call them *bala* markets. You don't know exactly what the name means. You guess it comes from the Arabic word *bila*, meaning old and shabby, but some say it's a corruption of a foreign word that you don't remember now. You've lived in several countries: there are *bala* markets in almost every country, but they can't be compared with those in the City of Red and Grey. In the *bala* markets in your country few people sell their own things. They are mostly clothes and shoes that come from abroad. The goods might be charity donations sent from rich countries to poor countries in the Global South, where corrupt hands, instead of distributing them to the needy, have turned them into a profitable business. In the City of Red and Grey it's ordinary people, not traders, who sell their clothes when they've been overtaken by fast-changing fashion. But they also sell various other things: crockery, music cassettes, electrical appliances, spare parts for machines that are no longer used, old stamps, personal letters, books that have been read only once, watches, compasses that don't point in the right direction, and medals from ruinous wars.

You don't usually wear a watch. You feel they're like shackles, tying you by the hand and creating a coercive bond with time. Time is not a watch. An hour is a unit of time only in car parks, on punch-card clocks for workers and in the beds of prostitutes. Time has other criteria, some of which you see reflected when you look in the mirror, while others appear in the length and pace of your steps.

You have been given watches on particular occasions but you would take them off and put them in front of you on tables in public places and forget them, perhaps deliberately, and when you went back to look for them, just out of a sense of duty, you didn't find them. Because people, even those who don't steal, love to find things. There's a thrill that's hard to explain about finding something that someone else has lost. When someone found a watch you'd left, perhaps deliberately, on a table in a café, hotel lobby or restaurant, they could have handed it in to the person in charge, but they didn't. You've never found any of the watches you've lost in the course of your life – to be fair, they've been few. You never doubted the honesty of those who found the watches. You would interpret the fact that you couldn't find them as a kind of inevitable fulfilment of your secret desire to lose them, although you are not fatalistic. Of course, that's having it both ways, but it's not the only case of that. You didn't usually regret any of the watches you lost. You don't remember what make they were or what they looked like. You would exhibit a certain insincere distress when the person who gave you the watch saw that it wasn't on your wrist. But deep inside, you felt relieved and liberated. It was another shackle broken. You were rid of that annoying tick. That was how you felt in general, but you were sorry, even remorseful, about losing one particular watch. It was an old wind-up watch that your childhood friend took off his wrist just before your hasty flight from your country. As he presented it to you, he said, 'I know you hate watches as much as I hate books, but the only memento I can offer you is this watch of mine. Please accept it.' It was a moving and sentimental moment. You felt, as he felt, that you would be away a long time and that you might never meet again. In your long exile you lived in several countries. You sat in innumerable cafés. You adopted a name that would be an additional cause of endless sleepless nights, and you never took that watch off your wrist – except to have a bath, because it wasn't waterproof. But you lost it even so. It happened when you were attending a literary conference in a country not far from your own, before you went back. You had put the old wind-up watch on a table while a number of writers and inquisitive people were hovering around. It was the first time you had done this with that watch. You went to the bathroom and came back to the table. The audience was about to disperse and you left the hotel in a hurry to be in time for an appointment with a colleague in a café near by. You felt there was something missing, something you'd forgotten but couldn't pin down. A few minutes later you remembered you had left your watch on the table. You stood up like an automaton and apologised to your colleague, saying you had left your passport on a table in the hotel. Only your passport was important enough to justify abandoning your colleague so hastily and in such confusion. Need one say it wouldn't have been a passport issued by Hamiya? Naturally, of course: Hamiya didn't issue identity papers to citizens who were in opposition or on the run. It would have been a passport from a government that was sympathetic towards the Organisation. Strange procedures such as that were common in those days. You didn't find the watch on the table. The staff had cleared away the ashtrays full of cigarette butts and the coffee cups that had accumulated.

You asked the receptionist if anyone had handed in a watch that had been lying on that table (which you pointed at), and he said he knew nothing about it. You asked the staff who were milling around in the lobby, some busily and some idly, and they swore on their honour (not an oath one can always rely on in these parts) that they hadn't found anything. After that incident you were given other watches that you didn't much care for.

You went to the flea market. That was before the plague had started to spread in a way that was hard to control. You had no particular purpose. Perhaps it was just habit, or what you would call, with a trace of your old ingrained lyricism, tempting stubborn fate.

You made your usual tour of the stalls that displayed clothes, jewellery, old records and crockery. You stopped at a stall selling antiques. The goods on display were not necessarily the property of the stallholder, who apparently specialised in watches and clocks and went to hunt down his spoils in towns far and near. That was his trade, and also his passion. That's what the man said, and it gave you the impression that there existed something like a 'clock cult' that brought together people of different backgrounds, something almost magical or religious. The man was an expert in watches and clocks. What he said amazed you, especially when he talked about the inner workings – the cogs, springs, hands, cases, faces, gearing, and the tiny batteries that make that faint ticking in a watch strapped unobtrusively to one's wrist or a clock hanging on the wall. A hive of activity, all coordinated, toiling away with stubborn mechanical persistence.

The time that you need passes in a blink of an eye, whereas you have more than you need of time that doesn't matter to you.

The slow time of waiting, and the fleeting time of
    happiness.
A time of stone, chalk and coughing, a time of air and
    drizzle.

Hundreds of microscopic metal parts intermeshing. Turning. Dovetailing. Overlapping. Working away tirelessly and thanklessly, under the enamel face. The man could have gone on talking for ever if you hadn't interrupted him by suddenly turning your attention to something else. Among the finds that he had placed in a glass cabinet, locked to protect them from the dirt or from theft, you caught sight of a circular watch with a large white face and a faded gold case. Your heart pounded. You asked the man to show you the watch. He halted his rhapsody on the inner workings of watches, of time and ticking, opened the glass cabinet like someone approaching an altar or going into Ali Baba's cave, and handed the watch to you. You began to inspect it: the large dial, the big Roman numerals engraved by hand, the long golden hands, the antiquated brown leather strap, the back stamped with the name of the manufacturer and where it was made. The hands had stopped at five to five. It had been a long while since you lost your old wind-up watch, but when you turned this watch over in your hands, it took you back to that hot summer evening when you left it on a table in that hotel lobby, surrounded by people none of whose faces you remember any longer. You told the man you wanted to buy the watch. It was expensive but you didn't bargain as you usually do in such markets, and when he saw you examining the time that the watch showed he warned you that it didn't work. He told you the company that made it no longer existed and that spare parts were probably not readily available, but he knew an old watchmaker who could repair it. The old watch-hunter winked at you and said, 'There you are. It's not every day you come across such a special watch!'

You put the watch on your left wrist as if it were a powerful talisman. When you went back home, your wife noticed it on your wrist. She knew you had once lost a watch and regretted it. You tried to hide your excitement. You didn't want to speak. You just told her that all old watches are alike and closed the subject. You knew she was starting to probe into your past, maybe because you spoke about it more and more as though it were a lost paradise. At that moment you wanted to be alone with the watch. You went to the bathroom. You closed the door. Inside you there was a mumbling that no one but you could hear. You wound up the watch but it didn't work. On your wrist it was more like a beautiful piece of jewellery than an instrument for telling the time, and you weren't interested in following the hands of time as they crept with frightening regularity across the world and across the bodies of humankind. You remembered that when you had lost your watch that hot summer evening the time was about five o'clock.

That night you dreamt three or four consecutive and inter-woven dreams, not all of which you now remember. You remember that you saw a thin young man with a droopy moustache standing in front of another young man, rather stouter, who was undoing his watch strap and offering the watch to the one with the long hair. He told him something you couldn't quite understand, but judging by the expressions on their faces, as they stood under a cloudy sky, it sounded sentimental and moving. Then you saw a wreck of a man, with some of the features of the young man with long hair, wrapping his arms around the trunk of a cinchona tree, look-ing startled by something.

In those dreams, which were tangled together like a ball of wool, you heard a regular ticking, and you woke up.

IV

The museums in the City of Red and Grey contain many arte-
facts stolen from your country and its neighbours. Some of
them are among the museums' finest and most renowned
acquisitions – the 'sacred goat' that was once a god, the vast
obelisk that visitors see at the entrance to the great museum,
the winged marble lions, the restored statue of the storm and
rain god, the 'spring palace' that was removed in its entirety,
and the stela on which the secrets of the first writing are
engraved. But, apart from these objects, there are few things
in the city that are connected with the world you come from.
For a long time no trace of your old country has blown your
way. You haven't met anyone from your immediate family or
any other relatives. As far as you know, no relative or childhood companion has come to the countries where you have
lived or passed through. Your family doesn't travel anyway,
and the people in Hamiya in general don't have a tradition of
emigrating or travelling. The City of Red and Grey has no
significant community of people from your country. There
are people you sporadically come across at public gatherings,
but you have started to avoid them, out of caution or irrita-
tion with their foolish rustic nostalgia. It never occurred to
you to live in this city, where many years ago your region was
dismembered like a cake at a birthday party. That never

registered on the radar screen of your imagination. You came to the city by force of circumstance after your ship ran aground there. But sometimes, in the gloomy tunnels to the underground trains, you see large advertisements showing the desert, camels, bedouin encampments and oases with palm trees, and underneath, in bold type, this phrase that never changes: 'The Land of No Rain'. You guessed that these tourism posters refer to your country, but they don't mention the name. Although you doubt that camels and bedouin encampments exist in the way the adverts show, the basis for your guess that the posters refer to your country is the wall of volcanic rock that appears in shots of the oases. But there are similar volcanic rocks in neighbouring countries too.

Hamiya has an embassy in the City of Red and Grey, but it doesn't do anything worth mentioning. It might as well not exist. Once, you remember, the embassy came out of its eternal slumber for the occasion of the historic visit of the Commander. It was because of his historic visit that you found out the embassy existed. You also found out that for many years it had done nothing but prepare for the visit, which was wrapped in secrecy until it was announced on his arrival at the airport. The Commander, by the way, was called 'the Grandson' for short, because his predecessors in the military dynasty were the Commander the Founder and then the Commander the Son, and the title 'the Grandson' never referred to anyone else in your country. He left his headquarters in Hamiya mainly for tours of inspection in the countryside or on the borders, and he rarely made trips abroad. The person who did that, when necessary, was his prime minister. It is said that the Grandson stuck to his office because he was frightened there might be a military coup against him, and also because he was a reclusive man uncomfortable mixing with others. But the prevalent view as to why he didn't travel abroad was that he was too engrossed in working for security and stability. This entrenched idea about the Grandson and his devotion to your security annoyed you, especially when you became interested in public affairs. Once, in the presence of your father, you criticised the feeble terms 'security' and 'stability' – which the official press carried straight from the mouth of the Grandson – as being 'imported ideas', and even your father replied that the man dedicated his life to work and was not known to have any inclination towards luxury or leisure. 'What's not to like about that?' he asked.

Then one day in the City of Red and Grey you suddenly found yourself face to face with Younis al-Khattat. The surprise almost undid twenty years of exile, with all the hardship and the homesickness, and restored things to how they were in the beginning.

With the passage of time and your wanderings overseas, you had almost forgotten Younis al-Khattat. You had forgotten his few poems, which were sometimes musical and sometimes grating, and you had completely forgotten the modernist metrical poetry of which he favoured the softest varieties. It's true that he visited you in your dreams from time to time, but dreaming isn't reality, as they say. Then, from beyond the walls of time and space, he popped up in front of you somewhere you didn't expect a messenger or good news from your country. It wasn't Younis al-Khattat in person that you met. That would not have been possible, because he never went beyond the borders of Hamiya. The one who crossed the border and left for other countries bore another name and was destined for other things. It wasn't Younis himself but his works, or more precisely some of his poems. A prestigious cultural institution in the City of Red and Grey had organised an exhibition of the arts and literature of your region. It included contributions of variable quality and importance from various countries. It was an event that was unprecedented, as far as you know. The world you came from does not usually arouse such interest in a large and ancient conurbation whose secret life is dominated by money, sex, questions of security and fading imperial dreams. It's the oil that gushes out of the region's deserts that monopolises its attention. That's the crux of the matter, as they say. Otherwise the region, which staggers under the burdens of the past and the pains of the present, which stretches – thirsty, hungry and humiliated – between the ocean and the gulf, does not exist on the map. Credit for this sudden interest in the world you came from must go to the suicide bombers that have given the people and the government such nightmares since the explosions of that bloody summer. It was the terrifying sequence of bombings, carried out by young men who paralysed a large city in broad daylight and amazed its inhabitants with their remarkable willingness to die, that made the elite take an interest in the principles and beliefs that inspired people to blow themselves up, along with other strangers. The bombings also gave the general public a phobia about people coming from a world wrapped in danger and mystery. Because life is dear in the City of Red and Grey, or at least it was before the plague broke out. In a way you find difficult to understand, it is cherished by those dying in hospital, by the blind with their sticks to guide them, and even by the destitute who call the streets their home. The inhabitants were terrified by

47

what the prophet of the bombers said in his message to them: 'We embrace death as you embrace life.'

The week-long exhibition was a mixture of older literature and arts, interspersed with some rather more contemporary culture. You heard of it by chance. You were living in a remote neighbourhood crowded with the poor – locals, immigrants and unemployed – and you seldom went to the city centre, which was noisy and busy. On one of your trips downtown, you saw a poster on a billboard in the main square, which was covered in the droppings of grey pigeons. The poster, inviting people to attend the exhibition, also appeared in the underground tunnels with their eerie lighting. It featured famous landmarks such as the Pyramids, the Pillars of Hercules and the Kaaba, alongside less well-known ones such as the place where Jesus was baptised, the Jalali and Mirani castles and the ruins of Mari, as well as fantastical drawings of men in large white turbans: perhaps distant ancestors such as Averroes, al-Hallaj or Haroun al-Rashid. The slogan on the poster was a saying current in the city: 'It's never too late.' As you read the poster you said to yourself, 'Perhaps it's an attempt to make up for the past, or recognition that the world extends beyond the clock tower that marks the birth of time from the clammy womb of misty grey.' But you were sorry that this sudden awareness of your world should have sprung from that apocalyptic summer, rather than from genuine curiosity or from an openness to find common ground, even common interests, without inhibitions or preconceptions. An awakening of that kind, if it had come about earlier, could perhaps have prevented the deep chasm that had now started to separate the two worlds. As you passed the poster, the words of which suggested a belated correction, you recalled a saying you had been surprised to hear from a politician rather than a poet or an acrobat: 'The most dangerous strategy is to jump a chasm in two leaps.'

The exhibition was indeed diverse and ambitious: amazing archaeological finds owned by the city's museums, recordings by prominent musicians, films from the black-and-white era, dances by men in white gowns and conical hats who whirled for ever, anthologies of poetry, a short story and chapters of a novel in both languages, and so on. In the anthology of poetry were three poems by Younis al-Khattat.

The name sent a shiver down your spine.

The large anthology contained poems by six or seven poets from your country, including a poet who was killed in a mysterious car accident. In the middle of them was the name Younis al-Khattat, with a short confused biography that suggested he also had another name. For ages you hadn't read the name in any newspaper or book, or heard anyone utter it. You had a recurring dream in which Younis al-Khattat appeared. Despite your wanderings in numerous countries the setting, content and words of the dream did not change. You were in a dark room with a raised bench where three men in military uniform were seated in red sashes, with ribbons on their chests. Next to each one lay an olive-green military cap decorated with an eagle spreading its wings. In front of them the rows of chairs were empty. To the right stood a metal cage holding a thin young man with long hair, a droopy moustache and shifty eyes. The three military men examined the papers in front of them and then looked up, towards the metal cage. Then the one sitting in the middle, the most severe and inscrutable, would speak these words: 'Younis al-Khattat. Life imprisonment.' You would wake up soaked in sweat every time.

You knew there had been change in your country. But you didn't expect to find Younis al-Khattat's poems included in an anthology of writings selected under the supervision of official institutions, for several reasons. Younis al-Khattat wrote few poems, and they were published in local newspapers with limited circulation or in underground stencil-copied publications edited by young men who believed that words could be as powerful as bullets. Besides that of course there was the fact of his conviction in absentia. It's true that the poems did bring him some attention in literary circles, and more than one critic wrote about the advent of a promising poet. But the fact remains that he was not a recognised poet, even though some of his poems on love and politics circulated among young people. One of the three poems in the anthology was called 'The Lady of the City', which was heavy with influences from the Song of Solomon. The lyricism in it is clear. The pastoralism – the hills covered with lilies, the lions and the spikenard – was also evident. But for all that clarity, a question obsessed you when you read the poem. How could a poet less than twenty years old describe how time weighed on his shoulders, how it had left scars on his body, how it made the ground sprout lily after lily and the gazelles give birth to gazelle after gazelle, and the days and nights pass in succession without his love for his beloved diminishing one iota? You told yourself that sometimes one's words can sing the praises of something you know nothing about or overestimate the permanence of feelings. They can immortalise a moment that soon proves to be transitory, if not pathetic. You also said that it is emotional and intellectual discipline that generally gives words a way out, saves them from the nonsense of their firm promises and makes it possible to read them again with as little disgust as possible.

You were not surprised for long that Younis al-Khattat's poems had been included in the part of the large anthology that was devoted to your country. While roaming through the galleries of the cultural institution that was hosting the exhibition, you saw your old comrade Mahmoud, whom you all used to call Abu Tawila because of his unusual height. Ever since middle school in Hamiya, Mahmoud had been noticeably taller than the rest of his colleagues. You were considered tall, but not as tall as Mahmoud. Those extra inches of flesh and bone were probably the only advantage he had over you. It didn't feel like it was ten years or so since your stormy last meeting. He embraced you and spoke warmly. He waved his hands excitedly. More than once he put his hand on your shoulder with disturbing affection. But you couldn't respond so obligingly. You needed time to cover half the emotional distance he had already crossed when he met you.

It was hard for you to forget what he had done.

He must have read the statement you and your comrades issued, which called him a defeatist who put his personal interests above the common cause. You were the spokesman for the Organisation and the one who drafted the statements it issued abroad. That was about ten years earlier. Mahmoud's surprise decision to go home had been less of a shock than his rapid appointment to a prominent official position in the media. Those who suspected he had been a plant saw this as proof of their suspicions, while others rejected this interpretation, which gave the impression that your organisational structure was lax in the face of other forces. They said he was just a defeatist, a petit bourgeois with no stamina. You were one of those who favoured the second explanation. If he had really been a plant, he would have given you away before you left the country: he had known where you were hiding before your escape was arranged, and when you escaped abroad, with some of your comrades, he was with you.

But it was striking that his comments on the nature of your work with the Organisation and on the rigidity of your theories had started only a short time before he suddenly decided to go home, and then only cautiously. He had started talking philosophically, in a decadent liberal tone in your opinion, about the relativity of evil. Comparing two evils: the regime and what he called the overwhelming tide of obscurantism. Within the Organisation you hadn't taken a clear position on the fact that the religious forces were vocal in the country and that some wings of that movement had turned to violence. You stuck to your class-based analysis of the regime, of the forces that had a real interest in change and the role of the revolutionary vanguard in bringing it about. You pointed out confusedly that what was happening in your country was a struggle within the bourgeois class itself. The right was attacking the right. But the thrust of your propaganda remained focused on the regime, which you held responsible for the conflict, for the violence and the bloodshed that was taking place. You said it was the natural outcome of its decision to use the religious forces to wage war on the left. You observed what was happening in Hamiya towards the end of the Grandson's reign with a certain vengeful satisfaction. What you didn't say in your statements, you discussed in your closed meetings: if the regime was weakened by the religious forces, was it in the interests of the forces of change or not? Your comrades were close to unanimous that in the end what was happening would work in their interests, because in your opinion the religious forces did not have a sustainable agenda. They were part of the forces of the past, and history could repeat itself only in the form of farce. By weakening the regime and shaking its foundations, these ahistorical forces would help put history on the right track, whether they wanted to or not. But it was a remark by the theorist of the Organisation that became proverbial, when he likened the religious forces to the ox that ploughs the land and prepares it for those who plant the seeds: the ox that pulls the plough of history. Then, as if he had had a sudden inspiration, he said: 'Let the ox do the work!' That phrase became an unofficial slogan. You didn't like the metaphor. You thought it smacked of opportunism in disguise, but you didn't say that, perhaps because the issue wasn't fully clear to you, perhaps because you were taken by surprise by the sudden change in the relationship between the religious forces and the regime. But you were not comfortable with what followed: the beginnings of a flirtation between the Organisation and the religious forces, to confront the regime. On that your position was unambiguous, passionate in fact. You argued for the need to stand firm at equal distance from the regime and from the religious forces. You said that tactics should not part company with strategy, and that it was liberal deviationism to say that the end justifies the means. But all this happened after Mahmoud had gone back to Hamiya. To be fair, you should remember what Mahmoud had said at the meeting where the theorist of the Organisation came up with the ox metaphor. He had ridiculed the slogan 'Let the ox do the work' and said the ox would turn its horns on everyone. Now you're wondering

53

whether what he did was make an ideological and political choice in favour of one evil over another, or whether on the Island of the Sun, the last place you had been together, Mahmoud had met one of the Hamiya officials who had come to the island for tourism and shopping; and the bargaining had started there. You don't know and you didn't ask him. But you could find no other convincing explanation for how he had managed to enter the country without being sent back, because he was one of a small minority of people that had tried to go home and not been re-deported by the border guards. Hamiya's policy in this regard was inflexible: not to let back fugitives even if they were wanted men, to leave them like stray dogs barking in the streets. This was the exact expression current in the official media when referring to opponents of the regime who were active abroad. The expression 'stray dogs' rarely meant actual dogs. Anyone who heard the expression on the radio or read it in the newspapers understood immediately what was meant.

Hamiya may be the only country in the world that does not arrest fugitive dissidents when they try to come home. Instead, it sends them back where they came from. This has created several diplomatic crises with neighbouring states as well as with other more distant countries. It once happened that a group from an organisation similar to your own left the airport on the Island of the Sun to go home, and the airport authorities in Hamiya put them back on the plane that brought them. The authorities on the island wouldn't let them back in and put them on the first plane back to Hamiya, and the guards at Hamiya airport sent them back to the island again. The authorities on the island contacted Hamiya, but the contacts failed to secure assurances that the group of returnees would be let in. Human rights groups condemned Hamiya's conduct. Statements were issued demanding that Hamiya let its dissident nationals come home, especially as some of them had wives and children. The appeals and protests fell on deaf ears in Hamiya, which forced the Island of the Sun to accept the group, who were kicked around between planes and airports until another country agreed to take them.

Many people know that this strange arrangement, unique to Hamiya among all the countries in the world, is the brain-child of the security-obsessed adviser, who is said to be a relic of a vanished empire, a man who does not appear at any public functions and whose photograph is not published in the newspapers; so shadowy a man that some people doubt he even exists. But those who are confident that he does exist assert that he was the man closest to the ear of the Grandson and that it was he who suggested this despicable procedure, which is a punishment harsher than the humiliations of imprisonment. The Hamiya authorities do not explain the procedure. They neither admit it nor deny it. But the most plausible explanation for it can be derived from the phrase, almost a slogan, that recurs in the official media: *Let them rot abroad.*

In his usual friendly way Mahmoud said, 'Let's go and have a coffee outside. Don't you know a good café where we can sit?' 'Sure,' you told him.

The cultural complex where the exhibition was being held lies on the riverside. Nearby there are several cafés and bars. It was afternoon. The great river that divides the city in two twists and turns like the body of a giant snake. Dark.

Mysterious. On its surface floats the detritus of human society – empty bottles and cigarette ends, just as the city's famous poet described it. Men and women cross in both directions, carrying umbrellas as a precaution against rain that might fall at any moment, their eyes fixed before their feet, oblivious of everything around them. You noticed that while speaking to you Mahmoud was ogling passing women in a way that violated the norms of behaviour in the City of Red and Grey. This is a habit that people coming from your world are forced to abandon grudgingly after staying for some time, because almost no one in the city stares at anyone, let alone casts lecherous glances at the breasts and bottoms of passing women. It's even worse for a man to look back at a woman who has already walked past him. This is wholly improper. When you see someone do that, you can bet he's a newcomer to the city, and you rarely lose your bet. That doesn't mean it's a virtuous city, because vice also exists, with its own market and customers. Vice is a packaged commodity: there are people who buy it and people who sell it. When you first analysed this you attributed it to capitalism itself, which commodifies everything, including the human body and human desires. Then you were uncertain how to categorise it, and in the end you saw it as a mixture of commodification and irremediable human defects. You don't deny that in the city you saw types of perversion you had never heard of before. Don't panic, it wasn't first-hand experience, but in the magazines displayed on the uppermost racks in newspaper shops (which you would sometimes peek into). From browsing nervously through these magazines, you learnt that there were devotees of feet, of shoes, of underwear and body odours, and that there were people who were turned on only by handcuffs, whips, canes and slave chains. Do you remember the Conservative member of parliament who was found hanging from a tree in a public garden, in women's underwear? People on their way early to work came across him hanging there, in lingerie, a conservative who advocated maintaining values and family cohesion. That made you wonder. Then you remember another strange incident that happened to you personally, but not here. It might not have been perverse but it seemed strange, and at the time you didn't find any explanation for it. Anyway, you hadn't come across it before. It involved a young widow, the wife of a colleague killed in the City of Siege and War. You had gone to her apartment to pay your condolences. You were surprised how the situation changed so quickly. From patting her on the shoulder, to putting your hand on hers to comfort her, to hugging her firmly, and then with desire, then with passionate kisses, and taking off her black mourning clothes and scattering them across the small sitting room. It wasn't the sudden surge of carnal desire that struck you as strange at the time but the words she used. In her husky voice, she asked you to have sex with her in the most explicit and vulgar terms. After frantic sex, and perhaps because of the vulgarity, which stemmed from a moment when you were both emotionally confused and carried away by raw instincts, she started to cry, almost hysterically. Sex without any preliminaries whatsoever. Unconsciously you were both swept away in its raging torrent. As she apologised, between copious sobs, you reassured her that it didn't matter. 'Please don't get a bad impression of me,' she said. She kept repeating this phrase until you left. Just as, in the heat of erotic excitement, she had repeatedly asked you to have sex with her in words that would ordinarily sound crude. This spontaneous erotic encounter with your colleague's widow was not the end of the story. When you again felt the urge to taste the unfamiliar fruit that unexpectedly hung within your reach, you went back to her. In fact you never forgot the strange squealing noises she made, nor the vulgar words she used. It excited you to go back to her, specifically the vulgarities of which you silently disapproved when you heard them for the first time.

As quick as a flash your memory came up with a much older reminiscence. One that was even stranger. From the depths of your memory there floated to the surface the image of an officer in Hamiya who, on a visit to the City Overlooking the Sea before a series of wars broke out, paid a prostitute three hundred pounds to piss in front of him just so he could see the yellow liquid pour out between her legs, or, as he put it, to see how women differ from men when they piss.

But all that is one thing, and the norms of public behaviour in the City of Red and Grey are something else. Call it politeness, aloofness or social hypocrisy. The appellation doesn't change the fact that staring at people and intruding on their private business are not approved of in this noisy Babel, where faces from all over the world ebb and flow, where people babble a hundred and one languages in the streets, bars and underground tunnels, in this conurbation that is tangible and abstract, simple and complicated at the same time.

You and Mahmoud walked past a group of young men and women who were standing in front of a fast-food restaurant, eating sandwiches and laughing together with infectious good humour. They had clearly come out of one of the offices nearby. Mahmoud pointed to the group and asked you,

'How's the invasion going?' At first you didn't understand. You hardly noticed the crude gesture he made with his hand but after a while you understood what his words meant and where they came from. He was referring to a famous remark by a fictional hero who came from your world: 'I came as an invader into your very homes.' For a moment you thought about the virility implied in this remark by the character, who turned his bed into a field of battle where symbols, natural impulses and eternal opposites fought it out: white and black, lust and revenge, sand and water, superiority and inferiority, Othello and Desdemona, strength and weakness, penis and vagina, hot and cold, Muhammad and Christ. An endless chain of binaries that met only across a chasm. An eternal relationship of collision and confrontation. In your opinion the causes lay in the nature of exploitation, not in human nature itself. East is not always East and West is not always West. They are not two parallel tracks that never meet. The world is more complicated than a railway line.

Is invading a bed, you wondered, the same as invading a territory? Is a penis like an occupier? You were not unfamiliar with the practice of likening occupation to sexual assault, to ravishment, because in your language you do compare the occupation of territory to rape. In this respect you may be unique among nations. You don't know of any other language that treats occupation as the equivalent of sexual violation. But, because of the drop of poison that the real invader had injected into the veins of history, the hero of the novel did not give free rein to his vengeful virility in front of the monuments to empire or in the corridors of power where the fate of nations was decided, but rather in the beds of the women who landed on him like flies. Landed on him like flies! You almost laughed when you remembered that phrase. Someone had used this tacky analogy when writing in praise of the fictional hero's invasions. Clearly the person who wrote that, or dreamt it up in his sexually repressed imagination, had never set foot in the City of Red and Grey. You had not seen women landing like flies on men from your world, or on anyone else. Did that ever happen in the past? When a face like yours was not often seen in the city, before such faces had become everyday objects, so to speak? Days when the East really was amber and incense, a metaphor for gallantry and ardent desire, to an imagination shaped by the tales of travellers and of people seeking a pristine world of wilderness and outlandish languages. Was there really such a legend among the people here? I have heard something of it: the echo of the legend even reverberated in your country among young men who had never left Hamiya.

You remembered the old files a friend of yours used to thumb through in his memory. He had come to the City of Red and Grey long before you. He was rather like the hero of that novel. He was highly sexed and lecherous, crazy about firm white flesh. He would salivate at the sight of the calf of any woman who passed by. Although you had nothing in common, 'the Hunter' (not his real name but a nickname you invented to make fun of him) was your favourite companion in long drinking sessions that were cut short by the last-orders bell that rang at a quarter to eleven in the evening. In fact this friend of yours did not come to the city as an invader or seeking revenge, but rather as a fugitive from a military coup, along with the financial and political elite of his country. He opened a restaurant serving Middle Eastern dishes in the city centre, and had his share of success. A perpetual bachelor.

Middle-aged but with the vigour of youth. He did not confuse his lust, which was insatiable judging by his own accounts, with symbolic revenge through the bodies of women. At least in what he said to you he did not connect the two, because sex for him was an act essential to life. Like food. Like water. The body's rhythm incessantly revived the need for it. In his case the motive and starting point for sex was sex itself. Or perhaps the pleasure of the hunt. It may have been chronic repression. You're not quite sure of all the motives that emerged from what he said. Sometimes you didn't believe the stories of his pursuits, because the hunt seemed much too easy. 'Hunt', 'chase' and 'prey' were the exact expressions he used: you would reject them and discourage him from using them, but he would not mend his ways. He would say, 'Forget about the veneer of culture and spurious refinement. Hunting is a perpetual human condition even if you wear the finest clothes. Because underneath the suit, or gown, and the neat hair there is the hunter and the prey, the male and the female, negative and positive. Men leave home in the morning as hunters, and women as prey. Men sharpen and unsheathe their weapons, women display the allure of the prey, cunningly defended. All our daily activities stem, without us knowing it, from this eternal root.' Your friend's stories about his sexual exploits sometimes sounded like fantasy to you. But you knew he wasn't lying. He might have embellished his stories but he did not make them up. You would ask him, 'So what happened, that people now walk past us without seeing us? Look. Here we are, sitting secluded in a dark corner that stinks of beer, and no one comes near us. We're like pariahs or lepers. That's not what happens in your stories about nights of passion.' He would answer, 'Firstly, you don't have the instinct or the inclination for hunting. Politics and culture have rotted your brain and distorted your senses. Secondly, I came to this city long before you, at a time when life here was more relaxed, safer, more carefree. There weren't these vast numbers of immigrants from all over the world. Most importantly, that horrible disease was still unknown.' You would later remember, remember for a long time in fact, what your friend 'the Hunter' said about immigrants, disease and fear of strangers. In the city's tunnels you would see large posters saying, literally, 'Don't speak to strangers.' Like most who come to this city from your world, your friend – with his old memories that he would flick through in the corner of a dark bar stinking of beer – had read that novel with the hero who cries, 'I came as an invader into your very homes.' In fact he knew the writer, who used to frequent his restaurant. He told you that the hero of the novel and the author had nothing in common. That didn't please him, because he had imagined they would share a common interest.

But you didn't come to the City of Red and Grey in the same way as the hero of the novel. Your personal situation wasn't the same, nor was his era your era. He came as a student, plucked from a tree at the height of the colonial age. You and your wife came as political refugees in the time of the nation state, when the authorities in the Island of the Sun asked your group to leave its territory, under pressure from your government, which wanted to make the world as uncomfortable for you as possible, to drive you away as far from the skies of your country as it could, to have you bark like stray dogs on cold and distant pavements. The difference between you and the hero of the novel was not just one of personality or epoch, but also ideological. Your idea of yourself and the world was different. You didn't start with the idea of two worlds that are always separate, always in conflict and that never meet, but from another concept, a concept of history as the arena for power, social classes and exploitation, regardless of skin colour, brain size, religion, or whether one is circumcised or writes from right to left. This concept with which you came to the city was a different idea you can call internationalism. Now it's called utopianism. Your concept has been shaken by the collapse of the models that tried to put it into practice, by the obsolescence that afflicts ideas just as it afflicts the real world, and by the fact that the journey grew longer and longer. But your concept did not collapse. You didn't want it to collapse, as so many other things had collapsed along the way. The idea that the concept might collapse frightened you, because you personally had no alternative, and because the alternative, at the broader level, was to have worlds that were set apart for ever and that met only on the battlefield.

But what of the fate of that invader who adopted the bed as the arena for his quixotic battle? He went back to his birthplace and disappeared entirely. As though he had never existed. As though the struggles he had fought in bed were just a quick revenge, fragile, recorded in police reports rather than in the annals of liberation. If revenge on the invaders took the form adopted by the hero of the novel, then the grandchildren of the judges and jurors who put that sexual hero on trial hoped it would stay that way. Then they wouldn't come to know suicide belts and men that embraced death in the way they embraced life. That's the form of revenge now: blind suicide belts, planes that crash into buildings and towers with everyone in them, and pound them into dust. No words, no greeting, just death floating on the scent of paradise, with dancing phantasms of houris in the afterlife. What's your stand on that fictional hero who invaded beds and cunts? What's your stand on those young men with suicide belts, armed to the teeth against historical subjugation, thwarted aspirations and the decadence of the real world?

When it started to take shape in your mind, you suppressed a question that countered what Mahmoud had said: 'Did you come to this city in defeat?' Invasion never occurred to you, neither in Mahmoud's style nor in the style of the fictional hero. What kind of invasion would that be? But why did you think about defeat? Your damned friend planted a seed of doubt in you. Whenever you dodged the question of invasion and defeat, it stuck its head up again. Your old friend's tasteless question and his embarrassing gesture towards the girls who were standing in front of the fast-food restaurant, oblivious of your existence, stirred an old question inside you, a question you avoided as usual by prevarication and obfuscation. It was the question that had started to nag like a whisper in your ear, faint but persistent, ever since you left the City of Siege and War. 'What went wrong?' it asked.

Mahmoud kept talking but you weren't following. He put his hand on your shoulder, as he used to do, and you moved your shoulder aside, out of his way. In the City of Red and Grey a gesture like that might be misinterpreted, because the men in this city do not touch each other. But that's not why you avoided his clammy hand. You were thinking back to the many days you had spent together since the two of you sat together at school in Hamiya, about how the two of you became caught up in underground work, and the dangers you faced in the City of Siege and War, where you lost six of your comrades. Apparently he had to ask you how you were several times before you noticed what he was saying. 'OK. Whatever,' you answered. It's strange how your feelings towards him didn't seem to have changed. But the way he spoke with such exaggerated confidence and gave the impression that nothing serious had happened to damage your relationship made you feel more detached. He seemed to be trying to get the better of you, and that irritated you further.

Someone who has lived through poverty and other ordeals, and has kept the flame alive through raging storms, would have a right to such self-confidence. That's the natural superiority of the moral high ground.

Mahmoud spoke fluently as usual, without embarrassment, as if nothing had happened. Your indifference and your dry tone had no effect on the flow of his words. 'I know you see me as a defeatist or perhaps an opportunist,' he said, 'but that doesn't change what happened in any way. Besides, the world has changed. The whole world has changed around us. Walls have come down, ideologies have collapsed and great powers have fallen. The old dangers have vanished, replaced by new dangers that are more frightening and more complicated. Don't you know that?' 'I know what I know,' you said. Then, as if speaking to yourself, you added, 'That's not the problem. The problem is that we left home together and pledged to stick together through thick and thin. You were not just a senior member of the Organisation, but also my friend. What you did was not just a betrayal of our cause, whatever setbacks it may have faced, but also of our friendship. That's what stung.' He said you were still utopian, and that his friendship with you had nothing to do with what he had done. There was no contradiction between the two. He said that things were very different now, not just in the world but back home too. He spoke about the importance of change from the inside, about the futility of travelling only for the sake of the journey, because the journey has to end somewhere specific, as he put it. He said that you wanted the journey for itself, more than the destination. In fact you may be addicted to it. When he said the last words you thought of that line by the famous poet, to the effect that it is better to travel hopefully than to arrive. You shook your head to dismiss the idea. Mahmoud thought you were objecting to what he had said. He looked you straight in the eye and said, 'Look. The Grandson is dead, and with his death a whole era is over. There's a new commander who's making reforms and opening the country up, whether from conviction or to keep pace with the changes taking place in the world, it doesn't matter. The important thing is that the iron fist is a thing of the past. It can't go on. The Organisation itself, at home, has changed its discourse and become more aware of the danger of the obscurantist tide, which hasn't been defeated yet, despite the blows the security forces have inflicted on it. Those reactionaries with beards haven't been uprooted yet. They're still influential in the street, trying to bully everyone else. Posing as spokesmen for God and his laws and working to set up their theocracy through violence and by denouncing others as infidels. I don't need to convince you that they're hostile to everything you believe in: modernity, progress, freedom of speech and belief, even drinking a glass of beer. You know that and more.' With one-tenth of your old comrade's enthusiasm and fluency, you said, 'I'm not speaking for anyone else now, not even for the Organisation, but evil is evil, with a long beard or with a close shave. I don't have to choose between the lesser of two evils for the sake of a glass of beer. Hamiya will not change just because there are a few former leftists in government. Anyone who understands the nature of the regime knows it won't change, because if it changed it wouldn't be what it is. It would be something else. In fact the ones who'll change are the ones who think they can change it.' Then, quoting a concept he must have known, you told him that to accept reality just by interpreting it differently doesn't mean changing it, but rather legitimising it. He didn't respond. Had he perhaps forgotten the Organisation's ideological training? Instead he gave you a meaningful look and said, 'Do you think it's a coincidence that the anthology includes poems by Younis al-Khattat? Haven't you noticed there aren't any poems by Khaled Rustum, Hamiya's official poet?' You didn't respond because you really hadn't noticed whether Rustum's name was there or not, and because you had never considered him a poet anyway, although the radio station was always trumpeting his pretentious and sycophantic poems. Mahmoud clamped his large hand on your hand, which was lying on the table, and you couldn't pull it back. Then, as if whispering a secret, he added, 'It isn't a coincidence. It was me who included Younis al-Khattat's poems and left out those of Rustum, who is now begging meekly in the corridors of official institutes, reminding everyone of his work writing poems in praise of the Grandson. Do you know why?' he asked. Without waiting for an answer, he added, 'Not because Younis al-Khattat is a friend of mine, but for reasons of creativity. We want to offer the world a true impression of ourselves.' I almost laughed when he said the last sentence. It sounded like one of those rants one used to hear in public speeches in the era of the iron fist, when fear was second nature to anyone who read a book or thought aloud, when petitions of eternal fealty, written in blood, circulated at artificial gatherings whenever someone tried to assassinate the Grandson. You remembered the chant of the mob: 'We are with you for ever, protector of the country.' You remembered the militaristic songs about swooping hawks, the men who drank the enemy's blood, the children who could sleep in peace only under the benevolent wing of the Father Leader, how everyone rallied in single file behind the 'Shield of the Homeland'. As if he had been eavesdropping on your internal monologue, he said, 'I know you won't agree with me, but I've come to this conclusion: it's people who make rulers corrupt, not the other way round. The rulers start their reigns afraid of people, awed by the responsibility. They don't know exactly who's with them and who's against. But the people, through their instinctive fear of authority and their automatic willingness to defer to the religious aura they attribute to their rulers, are the ones who turn them into pharaohs, Caesars, gods on earth: the opposite of your class-based analysis. Listen to this story I heard from the inside. In the beginning the Grandson protested against the excessive adulation, the panegyrics sung in his name. He told his aides, "I'm not like my father. I can't stand false praise and I don't understand these poems. I can't bear the guttural language with which they recite their poems. I especially hate those songs about my glorious deeds and the heroism of my army, sung in that nauseating rustic style. I don't want statues of myself in public squares or colour photographs of me in every house, nor operas on my birthday. I'd rather spend my birthday in the office or on a hunting trip. I want the people to respect me for what I do, not to acclaim what I haven't done." So he appointed a censor to throw proposals for sycophantic projects into the rubbish bin, without hesitation or

V

Hamiya is a real place, to the extent that places are real in the lives and imaginations of those who live in them. It was given the name because originally it really was a 'hamiya', a military garrison, a small fort made of black rock, with weapons and lean horses, set up on the caravan route that crossed this forlorn tract in the age of the far-flung empire. The area was rife with bandits and tribes that lived off raiding, and Hamiya deterred their deadly attacks for some time. Hamiya did not change, either in appearance, size, function or demographics, until the time of the ginger-haired general, but even then its name did not change. It survived in the same role until the empire declined and disintegrated. Hamiya's system of government is hereditary, or so it became. The constitution doesn't specify that the reins of power should pass down through a particular family. People hear about the constitution, the elite talk about it at length and the newspapers refer to it and even quote it, but it has no real substance. They say it was printed once, in complicated legal language that ordinary people couldn't fathom. But this probably falls into the category of things said about Hamiya that seem so exaggerated that they make its very existence subject to doubt. It was your father who told you, when you started to take an interest in public affairs, that the system of government in your country was not in fact hereditary, but more consultative, and when you asked him why power was confined to the family of the ginger-haired general, he told you they were the founders and guardians of present-day Hamiya and that their role as heads of state was in effect a tradition that no one contested. But those who reject this interpretation say the source of their power is the armed forces and the National Security Agency. That's how they have remained in power and monopolised it for so long. These divergent views on whether the system is constitutional or not do not appear to concern ordinary people, who have never seen a ruler other than a member of the ruling family, and do not expect to see one in the future. That's what they are familiar with and what is customary.

Only our ancestors remember how the ginger-haired general came to this area. Although they are long gone, they passed on their memories to those who came after them. The general chose the dilapidated fort of black rock as his base after scanning the surrounding expanse. After that, with help from the commanders of his small army, he set about drawing up an ambitious design, starting with about two thousand acres of land and ending up at about twenty thousand acres, or some say two hundred thousand acres. It was in the nature of Hamiya that it could expand beyond its core, or contract according to need or in response to the challenges it faced. The ginger general was a former officer in the imperial army and what he did was not unusual in those days. Similar things happened in other parts of the empire as it collapsed. They used to say that Hamiya's borders did not extend to the sea until a later stage, but this is not certain. A military man such as the ginger general could not have been unaware of the importance of having an outlet to the world. That's hard to imagine, especially as the old trade route originally led to the sea and this route was still used, intermittently, at the time Hamiya was founded.

When you escaped, Hamiya's physical appearance had already been stable for many years: there was the wall of volcanic rock, the lookout towers, the encampments of the various branches of the armed forces, the shooting ranges, the vaulted barrack blocks, the housing estates for each service, the large public park, the tall trees that lined the streets, the central market built in the traditional style, the public library with its dome, the sports halls, the polo field, the military airport, the large dam, the power plants, the model farms with their vegetables and livestock, the schools, the star-shaped headquarters of the National Security Agency, the devices that blocked the dust, the glare reflectors that tracked the sun as it crossed the sky, and so on.

Alongside the walls were massive cannons with long barrels and wide mouths, brought back by the ginger general from bloody wars overseas and painted a black colour that shimmered in the sunlight. The sight of them, next to the adjustable glare reflectors, struck fear into the hearts of the last remnants of tribesmen, whose only weapons had been short swords and single-shot rifles. In a way that left no room for doubt, the textbooks assigned to schoolchildren such as you asserted that the ginger general came from ancient martial stock, but this did not prevent a minority of troublemakers from casting doubt on aspects of the ruler's family tree, which was dominated by people with military decorations. Whatever the truth about his origins, the ginger-haired general, who was known among the people of Hamiya as 'the Commander', behaved like a father to all – a tradition continued by his son and grandson, the subsequent commanders.

In more recent times, when the cypress, poplar and cinchona trees had grown tall in the streets, in the military camps and housing districts, which were divided into square blocks, those who knew Hamiya attributed the decrease in raids and the disappearance of armed tribesmen to the awesome establishment that had begun life as a vague glint in the eyes of the ginger general. Others said the reason was the influx of traders, labourers and artisans, and the lighting of the streets, while others trace the decline and eventual disappearance of the tribesmen's attacks to the tribesmen's progeny, who were no longer as fierce as their fathers and did not have the same hunger in their bellies.

Anyway, Hamiya gradually subjugated the tribal raiders, with their swords and rifles, and took control of the surrounding area.

The population around Hamiya increased as people came in search of the work and security that Hamiya provided to the surrounding area. They moved into shanty towns that did not have the planning accorded to the square blocks, equal but different, of Hamiya's residential districts and barracks. The population increase on the outskirts began during the reign of the commander known as the Grandfather. It started to accelerate in the reign of his son and became a troubling phenomenon in the early years of the Grandson. These areas had no formal name but with time they came to be known as 'the town'. The districts that proliferated had no central authority. They were just communities governed by elders and strong men competing for dominance. Then, in the reign of the Grandson, they submitted to Hamiya's authority and together the two formed a combined political entity. But the name Hamiya still prevailed in common usage, while the official name was confined to government transactions. There must have been numerous debates in Hamiya about extending its sovereignty over these scattered communities. This is clear from the fact that there are contradictory versions of the relationship between Hamiya and 'the town'. Some people say it was the elders of these communities who asked to come under Hamiya's authority after a struggle between them came to a head and no one of them could resolve the conflict in his favour. Others say it was objective necessity that intertwined the needs of Hamiya and of 'the town' so closely that it was difficult to keep them apart, while others say that 'the adviser' suggested the idea to the Grandson, who – as a man descended from warrior stock – was not enthusiastic about it at first. The military life enthralled him. Discipline was his creed. According to this version, he seems to have feared that chaos, instability and the disruptive ideas characteristic of civilian life would seep into the heart of Hamiya. The Grandson knew it was his duty to safeguard Hamiya's supreme interests, whatever the circumstances. This was the family legacy, which would be in danger of extinction if he let down his guard and slept too soundly. Unlike his father and grandfather, he did not have friendly relations with civilians. He did not feel comfortable in their presence. There were civilians in Hamiya, running the municipality and the public services, but they were subject to military discipline. They even wore military-style uniforms, each according to his profession. Those who favour this version of events say 'the adviser' gave the Grandson sleepless nights with his warnings of the consequences that could arise if a powerful elder or an adventurous thug managed to unite the communities scattered around Hamiya into a single entity. The adviser's background in the social sciences, anthropology and astrology, before he started working for the Grandson, enabled him to detect social movements and rebellions, and to foresee the outcome, from his observation of the conduct of a single individual. No one knows for sure which is the correct version, because the minutes of the meetings of Hamiya's Supreme Council occupy a special corner in the Commander's archives, marked Top Secret. Anyway, the relationship between Hamiya and 'the town' probably began at the start of the Grandson's reign, and produced a single political entity. The Grandson was at the head, followed from the protocol perspective by the prime minister, who was traditionally from the elite of 'the town'. He was largely nominal and everyone knew that the Grandson was the de facto prime minister. But neither the Grandson nor his prime minister had as much influence over people's daily lives as the National Security Agency. Although it was certainly the head of state who initially gave the agency its authority it later became hard to tell who had the upper hand. No other institution penetrated every aspect of life as much as the National Security Agency, including the Grandson's office itself. This, at least, was the consensus among the opposition forces, both the armed and the unarmed, and it was almost the only point of agreement between them.

In your youth you had a chance to see the precisely geometric layout of Hamiya's extensive core, which you had not previously grasped. Only a minority of people, as far as you know, were aware of all Hamiya's facilities, because there were restricted areas, above and below ground. Once, and only once, you were one of the top students at the Upright

Generation Secondary School. The Grandson, in line with the practice of his father and grandfather, was in the habit of receiving outstanding students in his office to honour their scholastic performance, or perhaps to prove that he really existed and was after all a person of flesh and blood. There you saw a large photograph of Hamiya's heartland, taken from the air and filling a whole wall of his office. You were so amazed at how regular, how extensive and elaborate it was that you thought the photograph was a fabrication or a photograph of somewhere other than Hamiya, which you thought you knew like the back of your hand. The settlements that surrounded Hamiya and that had started to expand even further had left the eastern side untouched. They lay to the west, the north and the south, whereas the eastern side was open to the desert, to the howling wind, and to the remaining wolves and hyenas that roamed at night across an ancestral home haunted by beasts like them, and tribesmen on the alert for anything that moves. This dreadful void was no accident, and some people thought it was deliberate. A kind of strategy. The purpose was not to let Hamiya be surrounded, to leave one side open as an eerie space that would strike fear of the unknown into the hearts of all.

You are your parents' second child. Your brother Sanad is older than you. You were born at the height of the time of the big shiny black cannons. In the days of your childhood a space charged with fear and dread lay between 'the town' and Hamiya. You remember your childhood outside the walls. Your family lived in a poor neighbourhood at the end of the downtown area. Your father had an office there until he moved to work officially in the centre of Hamiya and took you there with him. Only the children of those who lived behind the wall enjoyed the distinction of crossing that protected space, and not the other way round. You remember your bloody battles with the other children. Your attempts to approach the wall, which were rapidly repelled by the guards. The furthest you could reach was the carpentry shop owned by the hunchback. Right next to that ran the covered watercourse that separated Hamiya from everything else. But this almost total separation gradually began to change when the economic elite and the political forces intensified their demands for more openness and for equal representation in the new political union. Despite the new relationship between Hamiya and the surrounding communities, the Grandson constantly refused to remove the wall of volcanic rock that separated Hamiya from its environs or to open up the gates where guards barred the way to any casual intruders. Only in his latter years, under duress, did he agree to relax the restrictions.

You didn't know what your future would hold. The traditions that prevailed in previous generations generally required that sons inherit the professions of their fathers. But calligraphy, the profession of your father and grandfather, did not leave a significant impression on you. It was your brother Sanad who was destined to inherit the family tradition, but in his own way and in a manner compatible with the needs of the time. He was born at a time when pure calligraphy was on the wane in public life, and there were new, previously unknown demands. Graphic design, for example. Your elder brother excelled at that and took advantage of the family heritage, although your father did not see him as a calligrapher, but merely as a designer. Your handwriting, on the other hand, was hasty and of poor quality – in ordinary writing, not in calligraphy, which requires patience, self-control, a steady hand, concentration, and an interest that you never had in inks and brushes with strange names. Besides, you saw your elders' infatuation with calligraphy and illuminated texts as a ridiculous attempt to restore the glory of the past and to bring to life an art that lay dormant in ancient manuscripts.

So fate prepared for you another future, another profession.

Another profession?

You don't know whether writing metrical verse in a modern style can be called a profession, but that's what you ended up doing. In spite of your passion for poetry, you didn't have a single book published, because what you wrote, some of which was published in the local newspapers, was not enough to make up a whole book in your own name. You would make do with this limited number of poems, not because the vogue for metrical poetry was in decline but because an unexpected event brought you by chance to a crossroads.

You didn't take much interest in your father's calligraphy pens – thick ones, thin ones, ones that looked like deadly arrows or like whittled reeds – nor in his Persian and Arab inks, his cloths and silks, or the smells of his brewed tea. His work, to which he was as dedicated as a pious dervish, irritated and bored you. Sometimes the past is no less mysterious than the future. Don't be at all surprised if someone gives you another version of how Hamiya was, with events, people and details you must have lived through but were not destined to know. What's new about it, or this is what you think, is that at the time you could not imagine a future for Hamiya other than the one suggested by the signs of power and permanence that were evident then, just as you never imagined you would have interests that would take you far away from your family.

*   *   *

81

Some twenty years after you left for a city overlooking a tame sea (and later to cities overlooking wild seas), you have finally come back to the place where you took your first steps. There were previously many obstacles that stopped you returning, including a life sentence passed against you in absentia. Although you're not now as interested in politics as you once were, and although you're engrossed in the past, in dreams and in seeking formal perfection in your writing, you know how deceptive memory is and how coarse the real world.

Nostalgia amplifies things. The memory preserves tastes and smells and images that are of its own making, or that are not as they were in reality.

Some people will jump to the conclusion that when, twenty years later, you went back to the places where you took your first steps, you did not find what you left behind. That would be a hasty and erroneous assumption. You found the covered watercourse as it was, except that it had dried out. You found the wall in exactly the same place, and the new communities surrounding it on the same sides were still there, greatly expanded. No spade had turned the soil on the eastern side and no concrete had been poured in that vast and fickle sandy waste. You even found Khalaf, the sentry at one of the pedestrian crossings into Hamiya, inside the wooden hut where his father used to stand guard before him.

Khalaf was your schoolmate in middle school, before he left school to work as his father's assistant. When he left school early, he said, 'You know I don't like studying. I can't bear books. I'm not like you, they make me depressed and more lonely. Since I'm going to inherit my father's position in the guardhouse sooner or later, why don't I do it now?' So you started seeing Khalaf helping his father check the identity cards of people going in and examining whatever they were carrying into or out of Hamiya. Books were among the things Khalaf's father scrutinised most carefully. There were types of books that were completely forbidden. Books printed in troubled neighbouring countries, which might export their troubles to you. Books that would poison young people's minds about Hamiya. Books that described the country in a way that was deemed unrealistic or portrayed it in a way they didn't like, such as describing it as a recent creation detached from its surroundings, or as an entity set up by a general of obscure warrior stock in order to act as the base for some inevitable foreign invasion of the region. As well as other books that spoke of revolution, of class and of man's exploitation of his fellow man.

What families feared most was that one of these books might fall into the hands of their children. Your father was among those who saw these books as a bad omen. He was in fact a reader, but his books were different, books with fine bindings and titles that were hard to read. Some of them were on calligraphy, some on Sufism – which you considered to be a kind of intellectual opium – and some were on classical poetry that was hard to understand, on poems in the *rajaz* metre, and on folk medicine; in other words, books that those of you in whom the satanic seeds of dissent had sprouted would – without hesitation – call trash. And since life holds in store for people a fate that they cannot know in advance, and sometimes brings them exactly what they fear most, you fell, unfortunately for your father, under the thrall of the most dangerous books.

Khalaf, your closest friend although he hated books, came out of a hut painted in the three colours of the national flag, now faded, with your solemn eagle spreading its wings in the centre. He didn't seem to recognise you. He stood in front of you, less erect than you had expected. He pulled into shape his creased blue jacket, from the belt of which hung a revolver in a somewhat shabby brown leather holster. 'Where are you going, brother?' he asked grumpily. Surprised that he didn't recognise you or even suspect that he might have seen your face before, you said, 'Don't you recognise me, Khalaf?'

'Sorry, but why should I recognise you?'

'Because I'm an old friend that you haven't seen for ages.'

He seemed to be searching his memory, which had grown sluggish with the years and with the intense heat. Then he resumed the attitude of a guard who shouldn't be too familiar with people he didn't know, and said, 'Your face doesn't remind me of any old friend of mine, though there is a distant resemblance between you and another friend. So who might you be, old friend?'

He spoke the last phrase with a trace of sarcasm.

'I'm Younis,' you said.

The name Younis isn't unusual in your country, so you had to add, 'Younis al-Khattat.'

'It's true I don't see Younis al-Khattat much, but you couldn't possibly be him.'

'Then how did I know your name?' you asked him.

'That's not hard,' he said. 'I've been guarding this entrance for about twenty years. Thousands of people know me, by face and by name.' Before he had time to send you off and go back to the shade of his ramshackle wooden hut, you said, 'Don't you remember when we – you and Salem and me – stole the papers for the secondary school exams and the Hamiya disciplinary committee punished us by making us spend three months non-stop painting the cannons with the secret paint stored in the depots of the Construction and Maintenance Department?'

'That doesn't prove you're Younis al-Khattat,' he said. 'There's a writer called Ayham Jaber, or Adham Jaber, who claimed in an article in a local newspaper that he was the one who did that. The newspapers aren't very careful these days about verifying what they publish, not since they laid off the censors who used to check articles and news reports for accuracy before publication. So that's no proof either, because the story was published, in a distorted form, and lots of people read it.'

'What about the watch?'

'Which watch?'

'The watch you had to wind up.'

You lifted your left arm and showed him the watch, which was ticking with the regular beat of a young heart. He looked at you for a while, then said, 'It's true I gave my watch to Younis al-Khattat, and the man called Ayham, or Adham, wrote a story about it in the same paper. But then in the old days all the watches were manual.'

'If the fact that I knew your name, and the fact that I knew about the exam papers incident and about the watch, don't amount to conclusive proof of my identity, then let me remind you of something else. You remember that Younis al-Khattat was severely punished when the Hamiya secret police found him in possession of a book called *The State and Revolution*, and he was branded with an iron cross on his stomach. That was out of respect for his father because, as you know, the custom was to brand people who committed such acts on the back of their right hand, so that everyone would know what kind of thing they had done.'

With an obstinacy that almost exhausted your patience, he said, 'But the man called Ayham, or Adham, published that in the same newspaper.'

Without further ado, you found yourself lifting up your sweaty linen shirt and showing him the scar of the cross branded on your rounded belly. Small, sparse hairs, some of them greying, had sprouted around it.

'Impossible,' he said.

'Sometimes reality is like that,' you said.

Khalaf's hair was greyer than you expected and his back, after forty years, was stooped more than usual for someone from Hamiya, where people often remain upright well into their sixties. The man now faced two possibilities: either he was dreaming in broad daylight in the heat of summer, or he had to concede that Younis al-Khattat, whom he had not seen much in recent years, was indeed this strange person who did somewhat resemble his old friend.

'How could you be Younis al-Khattat?' he said in confusion. 'You have balding grey hair and a thin moustache. You're frail, older and more careworn, judging by your face, while Younis al-Khattat, after that incident with the branding and after reading too many poisonous books, contracted a mysterious disease that froze his appearance as he was when he was twenty, with the same interests and powerful emotions. The doctors diagnosed it as a rare ailment they'd never seen before among the inhabitants of Hamiya. Medical delegations visited him to investigate the nature of this disease, which preserved his slender figure, his droopy moustache and his thick black hair.'

'I'm also called Adham,' you told your old friend, who used to ignore the books he found in your possession as you went into Hamiya, in spite of the gravity of the offence.

Khalaf no longer understood exactly what was happening. He waved you aside and said, 'Go away, brother, I don't have time to waste with you. I want to go back to my nap, which I hold sacred, and I'll miss it if you carry on with your riddles.'

But you didn't leave. You coughed more than once. You wiped your lips with the pocket handkerchief you were carrying in your hand and then hid it. Then you tried to explain to him, using all the memories you had to hand and all the evidence you could muster from your memory, that Younis and Adham were two names for the same person, or two names for two people who were once the same person but who then split in two after the book incident and other more serious incidents, because Younis stayed here while Adham went to the city overlooking a tame sea, from where his fates led him to countries overlooking wilder seas. You also told him that the person who used to write modern metrical poetry had lately became a writer of articles and biographies and had had books published in cities Younis never reached. You didn't expect Khalaf to know Adham, the writer of articles and biographies, except perhaps through extracts of his writings published in a local newspaper – writings he called allegations or fabrications about Hamiya and its characters. As for books, you knew his attitude towards them and you didn't expect him to have read any of them.

Khalaf began to reel from the existential shock.

He told you he was longer a guard working for the Hamiya government, that the Grandson had died and there was a new commander from the Grandson's family; not a direct descendant because, although the Grandson had been briefly married to a relative of his, under pressure from his father, they didn't have any children. (Of course you knew that and more. You knew the rumours about the real purpose of his annual tours of inspection in the countryside and to the troops on the front, which lasted the whole of the spring, and of course you had also heard of the resentment the Commander the father felt in his latter years because of his son's divorce and failure to produce an heir to preserve the chain of succession in his immediate family.) He said that one of the Grandson's relatives had been brought back from a military academy abroad before he had finished his studies, to take the Grandson's place; that the Hamiya he had known no longer existed, or, to be more precise, the contract for a project to develop it had been awarded to a large company that had started the transformation; that he was now an employee on a short-term contract with a new company that was going to lay him off after rebuilding and renovating Hamiya's infrastructure; that the company was planning to set up modern facilities and malls stocked with all kinds of goods, and was working on turning the houses of the officers, soldiers and civilian employees who had been living in Hamiya for successive generations into contemporary-looking flats; and so on and so on . . .

More distraught than he had appeared earlier, Khalaf told you that the authorities no longer banned the books that had given the families sleepless nights and that had led to the development of very thorough monitoring mechanisms in the departments responsible for national security and traditional values; and that those in charge now had a list of banned items that included books and other publications that dealt with such apparently contradictory topics as weaponry and computer programs. Now civil servants fluent in several languages kept themselves busy registering the titles and classifying them into categories, the most dangerous of which were the booklets on thick belts that explode automatically as soon as the temperature of the bodies they pass matches the setting in the electronic chip connected to the explosive charge in the lining of the belt. Now that he was reluctantly convinced that two people with different names and in separate places might be, for some reason that escaped him, the one person Younis al-Khattat, you told Khalaf that books lose their magic when faith in them wanes. They become just pale ink on paper. A book can be poison, or a flower, or a heart that throbs when it stumbles upon someone who believes in it. You also told him he had done well not to fall under the spell of words, which boast, sometimes deceptively, that they are the epitome of life or even life itself, while life, according to a writer who does not care to have his name mentioned, is somewhere else.

After listening at first in confusion and anxiety, Khalaf gradually began to take a genuine interest in what you were saying, reminding you of the days when you used to tell him stories or the plot of a novel that had captivated you. There probably isn't anyone who isn't fascinated by stories. They may not read books that tell stories, but for sure no one objects to listening to a story, especially if it comes to them when they're lonely or bored. So Khalaf thought it well worth listening to the story of the man who, to his misfortune, turned into two people, who were however reunited in flesh and in spirit when they dreamed or when they met face to face on the balcony of their family home.

Khalaf no longer spent much time checking the identity papers of those going into Hamiya or searching the bags of those coming out. He and his hut were just props from the past, because those tasks were now performed by modern electronic devices that saw through things, operated by unseen specialists. You saw people passing who didn't even greet Khalaf, people wearing uniforms and with plastic laminated name tags hanging from their necks. They definitely weren't Hamiya people or their offspring. You heard some of them speaking several languages, some of which you knew from living in numerous countries. Trucks and large bulldozers passed under the vast triumphal arch that could be seen from tens of kilometres away, inscribed with an incomplete line of verse. Khalaf was smoking a cigarette made in some foreign country. He offered you one and you said, 'I've given up smoking.' He was surprised. 'Younis al-Khattat is a voracious smoker!' he said. You smiled at the expression, which he had picked up from you, or from Younis al-Khattat, in the days of enthusiasm and promises. You remembered that he used to smoke local cigarettes that came in a square packet in the three colours of the national flag. You asked him why he had stopped smoking them and he told you they were no longer to be found. Khalaf sounded impatient that the story about the person who became two people was being interrupted, and wanted to hear it all, without any side talk or digressions. 'That was a long time ago,' you said. 'As you can see, I have all the time in the world,' he said. 'I've just arrived,' you said, 'and perhaps there'll be a chance later to tell you the story of what happened, and anyway, my story is like all stories, which tell of some things and are silent on other matters.'

'Here we are, breathing some new life into our old friendship, so if you don't want to tell your story, at least tell me who you are now. I mean, are you Younis or Adham?' asked Khalaf.

You told him, 'I'm both of them. My greying hair and my posture, which is no longer as upright as a strict upbringing in

Hamiya requires, are Adham, whereas the stubborn ticker (you smiled as you uttered the phrase) between my ribs may still be Younis. In fact it's hard to tell them apart. I know Younis stayed behind and, as you said, he hasn't changed much. But my new name and my new life apparently haven't turned me into a completely different person, and the proof is that I want you to come with me to where I buried Roula's letters and the perfumed locks of her hair, under the cinchona tree in front of our house before I escaped.'

Khalaf laughed. He still had his bushy moustache and there was a gap where two of his upper teeth had fallen out. The rest of his teeth were stained yellow by tobacco. Because of the two, or maybe three, missing teeth, he looked older than you, and you felt a deep sense of empathy with him.

'Why do you laugh?' you said, without disapproval. His bushy moustache, streaked with grey, cast a dark shadow on his lips. 'Don't you know?' he asked.

'Know what?'

'What happened to Roula.'

'Not much.'

'But Younis knows!' he said.

Then he looked at you with a trace of pity, or maybe of caution. You thought he was going to say you were like the bankrupt who goes through his old ledgers looking for debts he's owed, but he didn't. If he had, he could have wounded your pride, which was already wounded. You were going to say that you might be bankrupt but it was beneath you to leaf through old ledgers, because what was past was past and one shouldn't cry over spilt milk. You didn't say that, though he looked into the very depths of you, to the fragility that lurked there. You told him you were writing a history of

Hamiya and that your sentimental youth was a core part of the book.

With that mix of pity and caution, he said, 'You'd better not do that.'

'Why not?'

'Take my advice,' he said.

'But I have nothing to lose,' you said, without thinking what the words meant.

At that very moment you had a coughing fit that you tried to smother with the pocket handkerchief you carry around. 'You look tired,' Khalaf said. 'Would you like to sit down a while?'

'OK, let's go,' you said.

Khalaf shut the door of his ramshackle wooden hut and went off with you.

From the outside, because of the remains of the wall, the tall trees, the massive gun emplacements, the rusty glare reflectors and the dust blockers, the old installations looked the same as when you left. Of course you had expected them to look a little old and dilapidated, but you hadn't expected the public library with its dome, the vaulted barracks, the polo ground or the central market to be gone. Nor did you expect that the company assigned to renovate Hamiya would have started demolishing most of what was left with bulldozers and dyna-mite, or that it would all look completely different. Near the polo field you were surprised to note the disappearance of the iron fence around the headquarters of the General Command, where the Grandson had been based. The guards had been withdrawn; it had lost its aura of mystery and dread and been turned into a company headquarters. You saw young men and women going in and out of the building, carrying maps and long rulers, with mobile phones that never stopped ringing. You were surprised to find the Commander's new palace nestling, remote and stately, on top of the only hill overlooking Hamiya, surrounded by missile batteries and artillery pieces. You remembered that the hill had once provided the local people with a place to breathe fresh air when the heat was stifling, and had served as an arena for the carefree nocturnal frolics of young lovers, but in their conflict with the Grandson the jihadists had used the hill to bombard his office several times. You and Khalaf passed close by the Upright Generation Secondary School where you had studied. It was still there but was being used as a depot for the dynamite the company was using to blow up the deep concrete foundations of the stone structures. The name was still there, inscribed in a familiar *ruqaa* script on a stone plaque at the entrance, but underneath it the company had attached a metal sign with lettering written mechanically. 'Dynamite Depot. Keep Away', it said. As for the girls' school nearby, it had been wiped off the face of the earth, and it seemed impossible to make out the cobbled pathway that led to the park where young men used to date their girlfriends, under the pine and queen-of-the-night trees. Nonetheless you imagined a school uniform with purple stripes, a head of wavy chestnut hair and big dark eyes looking bashfully at a dark, thin young man with the sparkle and the mysteries of the desert in his eyes. You took the girl in the purple striped uniform by the hand. Your hand started to sweat and your heart raced.

Sustain me with cakes of raisins,
Refresh me with apples,
For I am lovesick.

You heard Khalaf say, 'This is where the Mothers grocery store stood, where you would trick the owner and steal the cigarettes she sold in ones.' You remembered the square packets of local cigarettes she used to sell. Khalaf carried on naming the buildings and districts that for a long time defined the real or imagined image of Hamiya, both for those who lived there and for those passing through. You could hear his voice as he spoke the names with a whistling sound caused by the gap left by the missing two or three upper teeth, but your hand was still sweating and your heart pounding. That hand, with its five dainty fingers, was still in your hand and the wavy chestnut hair sometimes brushed your face, and you could smell a mixture of jasmine and faint girlish sweat. In the meantime you thought about Khalaf laughing when you mentioned Roula and her letters buried under the tree with the perfumed locks of her hair, and you wondered what he meant when he said, 'Younis knows!' When you reached the site of your old house, its stones heaped up like a pagan grave, and you saw the enormous trunk of the cinchona torn out of the ground, you realised what his laugh meant. You didn't notice that your tour of the ruins of the old buildings with Khalaf had made you more like Younis than Adham, until you reached the site of your demolished house, where the teeth of a bulldozer blade had ploughed up the ground. You stood in front of the trunk of the cinchona tree, which you could once embrace with your two arms but which even four arms could not possibly encircle now. Four or five big slow scenes crossed your mind: Roula at your last meeting, telling you that you were still a child and would never grow up; Khalaf himself, avoiding looking you in the eye whenever you met; the

Grandson, shot in the shoulder, and the master of ceremonies shot dead; the poultry farm where you and several of your comrades hid, waiting for the smugglers who took you across the border one dark night.

VI

When you told Khalaf, 'I don't have a story worth telling,' you were lying. If it was up to Khalaf, he would have said graciously, 'Let's go and sit on a wooden bench in Hamiya Park and I'll tell you what happened today.' You could have done that twenty years ago too. In fact, that's what you used to do. It used to be other people's stories, not your own. You didn't have a story at that time, and anyway telling other people's stories is easier and living them is more fun. Lying to Khalaf was not pure lying. You didn't lie to him because you wanted to lie, but perhaps because you weren't confident of your story. It wasn't like those stories you used to tell him, sometimes on a wooden bench in Hamiya Park, sometimes on a chair in a café in the downtown area, or like the secret information Khalaf used to tell you about people arrested trying to smuggle banned books into Hamiya.

That's because Khalaf was in fact dead.

Khalaf had been killed before you came home, in a confrontation with jihadists who had adopted the shanty towns as the base for their activities. These people became active after you left and they came close to establishing a monopoly on the streets. They broke their long truce with the Grandson, or rather their undeclared alliance with him from the days when the National Security Agency was hunting you down like rats in holes. A group of them tried to infiltrate Hamiya while Khalaf was on duty at the pedestrian gateway, and he resisted and was killed. Khalaf was dead. You read the news, which was published in the local press, and you saw a picture of Roula, whom you hadn't seen since you escaped abroad, receiving the Medal of Duty, Hamiya's highest decoration, from the Grandson. She looked different from how you remembered her. Her hair was tightly gathered at the back, her face was severe, her mouth pursed and her dimples less pronounced, but nonetheless she had preserved some of her magic, which was hard to define.

You weren't alone when you escaped from Hamiya. You were a group. Most of those who planned the conspiracy to assassinate the Grandson and took part in carrying it out tried to escape abroad. Some were arrested before they could get away. Those who had played the least important roles were imprisoned. The fugitives were sentenced in absentia. The chief conspirator, the local leader of your organisation, was executed, and his relatives had to bury him in an unmarked grave. There were branches of your organisation in the City Overlooking the Sea. They were from an older generation than you. A generation whose ties to Hamiya had in effect long been severed. You felt there was a gap between you and those who hadn't set foot in your country for thirty years. They had the leadership positions. You noticed that relations between them and the people of the City Overlooking the Sea were not as they should have been. In fact that's how relations were between the other foreign groups and the people of the city, which had in theory embraced the cause of revolution and change. Those of you who had recently arrived from Hamiya and had just read the theoretical texts diagnosed the relationship as elitist. You wanted a relationship with the common people, not with the political elite and prominent people. The common people, or the masses, to use the phrase common in your political litera- ture, were the rock on which your struggle must be founded. They were the armour that would protect your presence among them on their soil. But for numerous reasons this did not happen. What your group had done together had created a strong bond between you. You were scarcely ever apart and you thought that what you had done had won you world- wide renown. A short time after taking refuge in the city, you were surprised to discover that few people knew where Hamiya was, although your country was not far away. As time passed and you moved around, the bonds within your group weakened. The warning signs of fragmentation began to appear at closed meetings and in cafés. Before the thousand-day siege of the City Overlooking the Sea, you began to argue among yourselves – over who was responsible for what had happened, who had informed on whom, who had lost interest and had turned to chasing the local women or was mixed up in business or smuggling, who still kept the flame burning for the cause – and this began to loosen a bond that had seemed eternal. After the siege, which drove you either to the sea or to the wilderness, some of you tried to slip back but you were deported. For years you haven't had any official connection with the Organisation, and after you left the Island of the Sun you all dispersed to various coun- tries. Your relationship with the Organisation became largely nominal. It was the leaders (in fact you had become one of them) who maintained a loose and vague relationship with you. They accepted your criticism. Your aloofness. Your moods, which have become more and more changeable. But they still see you as their protégé, perhaps because of your modest fame, perhaps out of loyalty to an old dream. You meet whoever's left of your old comrades by chance. At a conference here. A seminar there. You no longer hear much of their news, except that some of them have gone home and taken important positions in government. Obviously you weren't among them. After several failed attempts to go home, you convinced yourself that matters had become settled and that nothing could change the direction of winds that blew from just one quarter. But you did go home, in the end. You didn't find much of what you remembered. Change had not only swept you along; it had touched everything. Those who have been living abroad for years want everything at home to remain as it was when they left. This is impossible. You know that and do not often complain.

> You braced yourself to accept the cold, and the dark sky,
> The passage of time, the uncertainties of life, and the
>   treachery of friends.

But sometimes you cry. Some powerful force convulses you and you cry. Alone, beside a river with dark waters, you cry. Under a disused railway bridge, you cry. In front of the spectre who turns up at the worst of times, his arms folded across his chest, scrutinising you like an obstinate examiner, you cry. They do not last long, these convulsive moments, which might be inspired by an image that crosses your mind or a smell that reminds you of another smell, and you soon recover your composure and control of your emotions. This is a price you know must be paid, although no one seems to check the accounts any longer.

With all your self-confidence, your wounded intellectual pride, your deep sense of disappointment, your exhausted and sickly body, could you have said all that to Khalaf, if he were still alive? Probably not, although you're confident he wouldn't have gloated at your misfortune. He wouldn't have said, 'Didn't I tell you to stay away from those ideas, which only lead to ruin?' He's not malicious like that. You didn't tell him you belonged to the Organisation, because that's a secret you wouldn't have divulged to anyone, especially if you were arrested. You had received strict training on how to keep secrets and not to divulge anything important under interrogation. Khalaf knew deep down that you were no longer the person who used to tell him stories, who used to share secrets with him, including about your relationship with Roula, his friend who wrote love letters for the other adolescents in your gang. But how could you have told him you'd been chosen to check out the location where they planned to assassinate the Grandson, and to make sure the assassins could enter and leave Hamiya safely?

In the eyes of the Organisation you were very much the right person to perform this task, because you were the youngest member and the son of 'the calligrapher', whom everyone assumed to be above suspicion, and most importantly, because you knew how to get in and out of Hamiya without going through the checkpoints. You met all the criteria for someone who would not be suspected and from whom no danger was to be expected. You might add to that the recklessness that hovered over your head like an unholy halo. So the leaders of the Organisation decided to carry out an act that others had attempted before and failed. They set the date and zero hour for the operation.

The timing was appropriate: the celebration of the silver jubilee of the Grandson's accession.

This house has an arched stone gateway with an inscription in Persian script that irritated you for years. The house, to which you are returning after twenty years, was the family's summer house. It lies in an area allocated to the families of Hamiya's junior and non-commissioned officers and civilian staff such as your father. You lived there during the long summer holidays and your memories of it are partly good, partly bad. It hasn't changed much. The strange inscription on the gateway is still holding out against the ravages of dust. A new floor was added after your brothers and sisters had lots of children and finally moved in when your father was laid off. The venerable olive tree has grown and its trunk and branches have thickened. Now it reaches your bedroom window on the second floor, from which you used to see children playing football in the street, girls filling the afternoons with the scent of lavender, soldiers going to the front, and bedouin still attached to their scrawny camels. In front of it there now stands a supermarket with a foreign brand name, a hairdresser's for both men and women, and an Internet café frequented by adolescents whose long hair glistens with gel. But Antar, the dog that became devoted to you after you found him as a puppy yelping in the street and brought him up, has died. He no longer keeps vigil under your window or wags his tail when he sees you. Shortly before you came back, he stopped eating or drinking or wagging his tail. Your grandfather and grandmother, your father and mother, have passed away one after another. Your favourite brother Sanad, to whom you entrusted your boyhood secrets, lives in the Land of Palm Trees and Oil. Your younger brother, Shihab, the air force pilot, was given early retirement because they suspected his relationship with you might be more than merely fraternal. Salem, with whom you smoked, chased girls and daydreamed, and who became a National Security officer after you left, had a stroke and lost half his memory. Tom Thumb, who was your bitter rival in the gang warfare in the narrow lanes and who later became the leader of a feared smuggling gang, comes out of jail only to go back in again. Comrade Hanan has died. Salman, who first taught you poetry, has become an itinerant preacher. Your friend Hasib, who wrote detective stories, has disappeared from sight and is said to have died in a traffic accident while crossing the street drunk, or to have entered a monastery and become an ascetic. What next? It's hard to list them and count.

Nevertheless, in your room, which has become a guest room, you found books that had taken you away from your family, scraps of paper, official documents and sentimental letters promising eternal love. Among the books, which remained almost exactly as they were when you left, you reached out for a small book. Dormant memories of a distant age flooded back.

You opened the book and a multitude of sounds, images and smells swirled in your head. It was an inspirational book for you, and from the moment you opened it you were never the same person again. The moment you discovered it marks the unexpected dividing line between your old self and the new.

It was a magical book, but not magical in the sense of secret talismans, mysterious triangles or squares. It didn't have any of that. Its magic lay only in the fact that the words and images in it, its esoteric whisper, coincided with a willingness deep inside you to come under its spell. A susceptibility of this kind seems to have persisted in you for some time, but your receptivity to enthralment diminished the longer the road turned out to be and the less clear the landmarks became along the way.

As with any such book, you didn't have full control over yourself as the text led you from one discovery to another. Before you ventured into the expanses of that book you were yourself, but gradually you began to change as the book's subtle vibrations seeped into you. The first thing you lost was your sense of your own weight, then your old memory. The words in the book began to wipe out most of the words that were there before them. That's what you felt when you read it for the first time, or rather that's how you were predisposed to react, because you were fertile ground at the time. Seed sown in fresh furrows soon sprouts.

The book, which you thought you had lost in your apartment in the downtown area, took you back twenty years. You felt lighter, thinner, nimbler. You imagined your hair had grown longer, that you had a droopy moustache, feet that hardly touched the ground and eyes that reflected tall trees, blue beaches and girls from whose shoulders little panthers leapt. You recognised this feeling of being so light you were about to take off. You had experienced it before when you opened the very same book, brought to you by a young man named Hannawi, who was tall and thin with dishevelled hair and a slight limp in one foot.

Hannawi had come from abroad, and after you met by chance in the Black Iris café he became your best friend for some time. He was entranced by the book and for you the effect was contagious. The book was passed around among others, but its magic did not work for them. The book held its secret gifts within a cover that did not reflect the contents. You and Hannawi shared those secret gifts. Both of you changed after that. You changed for several reasons, some connected with the book, others connected with the workings of fate or chance, and maybe of volition. After you escaped you lost touch with your friend. You looked for the book in the City Overlooking the Sea but couldn't find it. You discovered you didn't need it anyway because the words now ran in your blood.

It was a poetry book. It had nothing in common with *The State and Revolution*, the book that had left you with a scar in the shape of a cross above your navel. You thought you were the only person alive in the world created by the subdued language of the book, its limpid images, its muted rhythms, the evanescent quotidian worlds it evoked. But you discovered that the book had changed others too. There were other people the book had transformed. There weren't many of them but they were slowly growing in number with the passage of time. They never became many. The title of the book was *A Prophet Who Shares My Apartment With Me*. It's a rather strange title. The strangeness lies in the juxtaposition of the words 'prophet' and 'apartment'. Prophets are usually associated with the wilderness and antiquity, apartments with cities and the present. So he was a modern prophet. Without a message. Without commandments that make people tremble. His revelations might be ordinary, commonplace, superfluous. The title of the book was in fact like its contents, and the author was a poet from the city of Sindbad who had lived through the noisy last century and survived into this even noisier century with the same vigour, the same scepticism and the same preference for seclusion.

Before escaping abroad you lived with your friend Hannawi in an unusually elongated apartment in the downtown area. You first encountered the book when he pulled a cheap modest paperback edition of it from his bag, which didn't hold much, and read you some lines of poetry in free verse with a muted rhythm that was cunningly insidious. As he read, your friend's voice was moving. He was like someone reading to himself. He didn't know that the words were sinking into you and coming to rest somewhere deep inside that had been waiting since you don't know when. As he concentrated on the book, in his eyes you saw water rippling, arches swaying and skies rising, with sad palm or cypress trees. Your friend Hannawi was like the man who lived with the narrator of the poem in the book, also in an elongated apartment. You thought it was just a coincidence. But nonetheless you did feel that, several years earlier, someone far away had looked down upon your future life and written it up. Here was someone who had said things that you wanted to say but still didn't know how. When Hannawi had finished reading the poem, you said, 'Give me that book.' You went to the Black Iris café that you frequented in the downtown area, sometimes with Khalaf, telling him stories, and sometimes with Hannawi, reading what the two of you had written or talking about books that might have changed other people but not you two, which in fact might have bored you. In the café you saw Hamed Alwan the poet sitting in his usual place in the middle. Your relationship with him was a mixture of love and hate. You liked the direct way he spoke, his daring approach to criticism, his surprising ideas, but you hated his biting sarcasm about your younger generation's taste for what he called the gimmicks of modernity. He believed in direct poetry. Poetry that would move the masses and provide them with a weapon against injustice and tyranny. He was famous. He had a following that memorised many of his protest poems. Maybe that was another reason why you hated him; or, more precisely, it made your relationship with him more ambiguous. As soon as you came in he invited you to a cup of coffee. At the time you only wanted to be alone with the book. Nothing else. But you would have been embarrassed to turn down his invitation. He saw the book in your hand. He took it without asking. He read the title aloud: *A Prophet Who Shares My Apartment With Me*. He laughed his famous laugh. His raucous laugh. He examined it quickly and handed it back to you. Strangely, he said, 'An excellent book. I've read it. But his voice is more muted than it should be. I met the author at a poetry festival in the city of Sindbad. An admirable man but not impressive.' His opinion surprised you. You had thought he would heap scorn on him without mercy. Hamed Alwan laughed aloud again and, speaking in his irritating rustic manner, said, 'You look spooked.' You didn't know what he meant but you laughed along with him. You didn't want to have a long conversation. Fortunately Alwan left the café for a prior engagement, or so he said, and you remained alone with the book.

How many times do you have to change?

How many times do you have to come across what you're looking for, and when you find it, it's not it?

A year earlier you had read a book that spoke of rain and sadness and impossible love. You remember the rain more than anything else. Heavy rain would fall on you steadily as you were walking down a side street to your house in Hamiya. You would arrive drenched and your family couldn't understand where the water had come from when the air was so dry. You came back from the café after you don't know how long and said to Hannawi, as if resuming a conversation that had been interrupted two minutes earlier, 'Tell me more about the author of this book. Is he in the city of Sindbad?' He said he was probably there, because he never left the shade of the palm trees. 'I'd like to see him one day,' you said. 'Maybe you'll see him,' he said. Then he added, 'What matters is the book, not the author.'

These memories came back to you as you leafed through the book, which had stood in your old library as if you had left it there the day before. Memories of the Black Iris café came back too, and of Umara Street and of the apartment where you lived with Hannawi; memories of Hamed Alwan (who was killed years ago in a mysterious car accident) laughing his raucous laugh, and of the mission you were assigned, to convey a secret message to the leadership of the Organisation abroad; and memories of how you changed the company you kept whenever you met a group of people closer to your changing interests. You saw yourself as a slim young man with long hair, a tight shirt and flared trousers, driving through towns and villages and across the desert in a taxi every part of which was red hot – the body, the windows and even the door handles. Then you remembered the street where you had stayed in a small hotel and the room where a large ceiling fan had stirred the viscous air with an audible groan. And the three days you had spent there, waiting for a messenger from the founder of your organisation to take the message you had carried in a secret compartment in one of your high-heeled boots, then how you slipped out into the street when you could no longer bear the boredom, the fierce sunlight that hit you as soon as you left the hotel, and the bookshop you went into at the end of the street.

In one of your boots was a secret message of unknown content, and in your head were poems with a subdued tone that your father, a reader of the classics, would not have considered poetry worthy of the name. Printed on the cover of his book, the picture of your favourite poet, who rarely gave interviews to newspapers or magazines, was etched in your mind.

You asked the man who seemed to be the owner of the bookshop about your favourite poet, and he said that he was in the city but that he didn't know him personally. Then he added with a smile, as though colluding in a secret, 'A new book of his has come out!' He went into the dark depths of the bookshop and came back bearing a book with a black cover on which was written in a common newspaper-style *naskh* script: *A Star for a Future Evening*. It was about one o'clock. You were the only customer on that scorching August afternoon. The shopkeeper invited you to have a glass of tea. He went out into the shimmering heat of the street and came back dripping with sweat. Behind him came a boy dressed in a long white apron with permanent tea stains, carrying a small silver tray with two delicate glasses decorated with Persian miniatures. The bookshop owner, with the same conspiratorial smile, asked if he could try one of your cigarettes. You were smoking a cigarette made of your country's best tobacco, a cigarette called Alexander after the Greek commander who passed through your country, or nearby. The bookshop owner took a deep puff, held it down, then slowly exhaled. He told you he had obtained a packet of these cigarettes from a student from your country who was studying there and that he liked them very much. Then, with a trace of contempt that annoyed you, he said, 'How is it that you, an upstart country, can make cigarettes that are much better than our cigarettes, which taste like sawdust?' You didn't answer him. You told him you were interested in the author of the book. He pointed to a wooden newspaper rack near the entrance and said, 'He writes for that newspaper.' There were many newspapers in the wooden rack, and you couldn't tell which one the shopkeeper was pointing at. He stood up and brought over a newspaper with a red logo that included a hammer and sickle. You examined the newspaper, which had very few pages. It looked different from the other papers. But there was nothing in it by your favourite poet. The shopkeeper said he did write for it, but not every day. Then he said he didn't know which day he wrote, but he definitely did write for it. You were in a hurry to leave. You wanted to go to the hotel to read *A Star for a Future Evening*. You also wanted to buy the newspaper, but, with a note of caution he hadn't shown until then, the shopkeeper said, 'You're a stranger in this city. I wouldn't advise you to carry the newspaper with you.' You said, 'But it's not a secret newspaper, is it?' 'It's not underground,' he said, 'because here I am selling it with the other papers, but . . .' (he looked around him and lowered his voice) 'but there are people who monitor those who buy it.'

You left the newspaper, based on the shopkeeper's advice, especially as you were on a secret mission in the city, and besides there was nothing in it by your favourite poet. You thought how strange it all was: the founder of your organisation was living as a political refugee in a country that monitors people who buy a newspaper! You said to yourself: 'What's the difference between the city of Sindbad and Hamiya?' You didn't bother too much about the idea. You had something more important in mind. You rapidly retraced your steps, under a sun that melted the asphalt, to your hotel that faced a small bronze statue standing in the middle of the street in complete isolation. *A Star for a Future Evening* was an extension of the first book you had read by the author. You started reading passages of it aloud, then repeating them, unconcerned that the messenger was late in coming to collect the message folded inside the secret compartment in one of the boots you had thrown on the ground next to the bed.

You didn't see the poet on that visit. But you took this book of his back to Hannawi, who thought it less important than *A Prophet Who Shares My Apartment With Me*. You disappeared for some time, you and Hannawi, and you turned up again by chance in the city that would see a long war and a total siege that lasted a thousand days. You didn't forget the poet despite the bullets that flew past. You said to your friend Hannawi, 'I'll go and see him.' You did go, but by plane this time, and you saw the owner of the bookshop.

You had brought him a carton of the foreign cigarettes and some local arak. 'Ah, you?' he said. 'Yes, me and not me,' you said. 'You seem rather different, but what are these riddles: me and not me?' he said. 'That's another story,' you told him.

You found out that your favourite poet hadn't had a new book published, that he was no longer writing for that newspaper and that he was working in 'the palm laboratories' amid pollen dust and hybrid seedlings. You went and saw him. He was taller than you expected, thin, with a moustache streaked with grey. He was biting on a pipe that had gone out and he took it out of his mouth from time to time to look into the bowl. You never saw him light it or put any tobacco in it. You thought that the gesture of taking the pipe out, looking into it and then putting it back between his lips, or rather his clenched teeth, was a deliberate device to avoid talking with you. Your favourite poet didn't talk much. He wasn't what you had expected or how you would have liked him to be. He didn't believe you had come specially to see him, from a city at constant war, where the airport was rarely open. He didn't say that, but you sensed his mistrust deep down. You imagined, because he was under surveillance, that he had doubts about the nature of your visit, even though you weren't from his country and had nothing to do with its politics. The author of *A Prophet Who Shares My Apartment With Me* seemed distracted, remote, listless, although you recited one of his poems to him from memory. He may have thought your visit was a trap to draw him out of the cocoon that he had closed tight around himself. You would find out later that such suspicions were a trait deeply ingrained in the city of Sindbad. The succession of military brutes that ruled the country had planted eavesdropping devices almost everywhere and had persuaded children to spy on their parents. His poetry had a magic that was more powerful than his wary personality and what he said, half of which he mumbled. But you understood him nonetheless. You understood that he had put his best into the words he wrote and not into the words he spoke, and this does happen.

VII

Hamiya came first, but once the stone wall had been built it wasn't long before the first shop opened in the downtown area. This detail is important: apart from that, society vouches for the rest of the details, which are hard to enumerate. Your father knows how the covered market began. Before that there were shops scattered here and there, built out of concrete blocks that were not commonly used at the time. He also knows the owner of the covered market, which was named after the man. You used to make forays into that shady, tunnel-like, half-dark market, which was hardly wide enough for someone going in to squeeze past someone coming out (so much so that men and women sometimes contrived to meet there, in the knowledge that they could safely come into close contact in a way that outside the market would have been scandalous enough to merit a flogging). Close to the gateway to the covered market, the Black Iris café began as a wooden stall selling tea and coffee. The stone building was built later on the same spot. You heard this detail from your father, because you knew the café only when it was already thriving.

It was the first café you sat in as a young man. You would read there. Smoke. You'll never forget the metal board with the name 'Mr Ihsan al-Shatti' written in a modern *naskh* script. You and your peers all thought that Ihsan was only a woman's name, but then you discovered it could apply to both males and females. And here was the proof: Mr Ihsan al-Shatti, whom you knew as a man of medium height, stout, with a white face and short soft hair parted to the right and streaked with grey. He shaved once or twice a week and always wore a white shirt and tightly fitted black trousers. He was helped in the café by his son Taysir, who was four or five years older than you. To be free of the misery of school and school books, you would have liked to be Taysir. His age. With his freedom to smoke. His ability to buy a cinema ticket from his own money. To work all day alongside his tolerant, easy-going father. Your father wasn't cranky or irascible. But when it came to studying and learning he was stricter than his chess partner, Mr Shatti.

The café was still in the same place. It's true it had grown shabbier, but the metal board, penned by your father, was still at the entrance, coated with soot from the exhaust pipes of vehicles and the emissions of small workshops that were holding out against the ravages of modernisation. There was no sign of Mr Ihsan al-Shatti. There was a man of about the same height, the same stoutness and the same complexion, with the same hairstyle. It was Taysir. He saw you, stared at you a while, but did not seem to recognise you.

When you were living in a rough neighbourhood at the edge of the downtown area, your father used to sit in this café after finishing work. In summer he would have a mint tea, in winter tea with cinnamon and ginger. He would take a break from his pens and inks and from the phantoms of a thousand calligraphers in his head, or play chess with Mr Shatti. During work hours he would order his coffees and teas from the café, for himself and his many guests, sometimes delegating you for this task if Hassan the office boy had work outside. Your father would repeat his orders to you item by item. He knew your head was always somewhere else, ready to respond to any invitation to play or take part in 'devilry', as he put it. Mr Shatti would see you rushing about, ready to take off, and would repeat his standard phrase without the slightest variation: 'How's the young calligrapher?'

Like anywhere that's full of life, the downtown area grew crowded, even clogged, with people, with traffic and smells. In spite of everything, in spite of rampant modernisation, of time riding roughshod over the old, and the growing divide between rich and poor among the local people, it still formed the guts of the town and the stem from which the other districts extended like tentacles into the surrounding plains and valleys, in all directions except the east, which was left to the eerie desert. The function of this downtown area had not changed, but the faces and the appearances of those who frequented it may have changed. This is what you noticed when you were hanging around among the crowds there after you went back. You also noticed that the people you still know here rarely go there, now that fancier and more modern shopping areas have sprung up in places far from the crowds. You noticed with surprise that there were large numbers of foreign tourists, who are usually drawn to narrow streets crowded with pedestrians and goods, with strong scents and the street cries of people selling spices, vegetables and fruit. There weren't any tourists before. At least, you don't remember there being any. It hadn't occurred to you to wonder about that at the time. Perhaps because the Hamiya authorities imposed restrictions on tourism, just as they imposed restrictions on travel abroad, or perhaps because in those days the place didn't yet have a past that was disappearing. Now there were many tourists, most of them from faraway countries. You could see the amazement on their faces when they saw that local goods were still on sale, in a world where commodities and other things have been standardised and individuality is the exclusive preserve of museums and antique shops.

You were with your son Badr, who was named after a poet you liked in your early youth, though he didn't become a poet but rather a student of architecture. Your return to your country was not some figment of your imagination. This was demonstrated to you in an email you received from your friend Ghaith, who was enthusiastic about existential literature and aroused your interest in it too. He was commenting on your impressions of your return and of your tour downtown. It's clear that you had written an article about your visit on the website you contribute to from time to time in the City of Red and Grey. Here's an extract from Ghaith's email: 'Your article oozes nostalgia. It's the nostalgia felt only by those who have felt the pain of departure. The days add up and one's resolve flags the longer one journeys. The article is the work of someone who turned his back on home and set out to look for truths elsewhere. But, if only you knew, they are not there. This is what we don't know at the beginning of the journey, because the truths are here. Inside us. Inside our yearning to know more about ourselves. Inside the old markets where we have left stuff that might have guided us to ourselves. You wonder whether we can live up to our big words and bring to fruition the promises we have sown like seeds. This implies guilt, and guilt serves no purpose. By writing this you are avoiding the real objective. Posing the wrong question. So you won't find an answer, or maybe you'll get a misleading answer. The reality you have seen doesn't provide the answer you seek, and neither does your hectic tour of your old haunts with your son bring the truth closer. You may have gone back, but you haven't arrived.'

It wasn't you who wrote these words. Clearly. But they are proof that you published an account of your tour on a well-known website that is followed by many, including your friend Ghaith. Ghaith found solace in books similar to your father's, or so he told you in his message after some foreign trip (to use his expression), but not one as long as yours. One proof that the previous words are not yours is that he says, 'The truth is inside us!' Those are words with a religious flavour, and that's not your tone, because religion, as you would counter with a poetic flourish of your own, is a dark cloud that blurs the distinctions between everything in existence. It's a single package and you must either take it or leave it.

You think there's an inner truth and an outer truth. The two truths might merge, they might change places but they cannot be the same thing. In your view reality comes before the idea: first reality, then the idea. The idea is the offspring of reality and cannot exist without it. This is not your invention, but what you have read in books that cast a spell on you, and believed. Anyone familiar with your quarrels with your father knows you fought a relentless war with him against the idea that the inner truth reflects a higher truth that is the source of all truths. You weren't convinced that there is one supreme source of truth. One form from which all other forms are derived. You believed it was people who invented the absolute, supreme and total truth, so that their final resting place, from which they could never escape, would not be in the dust. It was the need for solace, or a longing to come back again. Human narcissism. But there is no return from dust and decay. No Day of Assembly. No resurrection. No heaven and no hell. Your father would block his ears when he heard you uttering one of these blasphemous noes. 'I take refuge with God from the accursed devil,' he would say. But what your friend Ghaith said is no less confusing than the argument by which you try to prove that your visit to the old market happened a short while ago 'in reality', and not in a dream, not in the remote past or in an uncertain future; and that Badr, the enthusiastic student of architecture who shares some of your traits, but not your nervousness or your tendency to melancholy, was with you in that sudden heatwave.

To emphasise the point, this is what happened:

You were sitting with Badr in the Black Iris café, which is in Umara Street, sipping mint tea served to you by a waiter from an old country to which history has been unkind, who was trying, without noticeable success, to talk to his customer in your local dialect. You had come to this café after having your hair cut in a small barber's shop a few steps down the street. You used to know the owner of the barber's shop, but he seems to have retired or died and the young barber might be his son, but you didn't ask, to avoid a conversation that would have dragged on and pleasantries you're not good at. Between rapid and skilful snips of his scissors, the young barber was following a football match between a local team and an Asian team in the knockout stages of a continental cup. There were some young men of his age in the shop. Clearly friends of his, they were riveted to the television screen in excitement as they watched the local team take the lead over the Asian team. The match was not yet over when the barber finished cutting your hair, and the local players still held the lead. You left the barber's shop into a surprise hot blast. The weather was hot, very hot. You didn't notice but the heat made it look like there was a curfew. You and Badr were walking almost alone down the street, which shimmered in a scorching haze.

You know this long street. You have many images of both sides stored in your memory. They include the image of a pair of feet in tattered running shoes cutting their way through it like a 'drunken ship'. But you don't remember sitting in a café on the eastern side of the street. Perhaps because there wasn't a café there, or because you usually sat in the Black Iris café.

While you were walking down Umara Street, you ran into Fahmi, a writer of science fiction stories who was with you in the city where you took refuge after escaping from Hamiya. Although he was with you there, he wasn't part of your group or of your generation. He belonged to an older group, most of whom had fled abroad like you. You hadn't seen Fahmi since the siege of a thousand days, but he hadn't changed much anyway. He was carrying the small bag you used to see him carrying in the 1970s. He laughed when he saw you, and something golden glinted in his mouth. Perhaps the remains of a gold tooth. Fahmi was surprised to see you here and when you invited him for a cup of coffee in the Black Iris café, he said he couldn't because he had an urgent appointment and that you were bound to meet again, given that you had finally come home. Badr asked you who this man was that you greeted with a warmth you hadn't previously shown, and you told him he was a writer. You told him, as far you could remember, about one of his fantasy stories in which pieces of a satellite fell on a city with glass towers that were protected by robots. It was a story known to most of those who used to sit in the cafés of the City Overlooking the Sea. Badr didn't think the subject of the story was strange, though it was strange at the time it was published.

When you and Badr sat down at the table, part of the rough area where you used to live with your friend Hannawi was visible in front of you. As you tried to identify a particular spot in the area, you told Badr that in the distant past you had lived in an unusually elongated apartment on the roof of a building there. He was surprised. But it wasn't surprising. Badr, the student of architecture, tried to sketch the houses piled on top of each other where you lived, when you were about his age, in an apartment behind a maze of washing lines, where clothes of a hundred and one colours fluttered in the breeze. He showed you the sketch and you saw a scene that started with the shops right in front of you, selling meat, mobile phones, clothes, vegetables and coffee, and then ending in open sky where three kites made of coloured paper were flying high. Three kites that defined the horizon, tumbling and turning alone in the void, while the children flying them (for that's probably who they were) were invisible among the houses, which from a distance looked like pale cardboard boxes.

The café, protected by the thick stone blocks of its walls and aired by a large ceiling fan, had retained some of its cool-ness despite the stifling heatwave. The cafés in the downtown area still performed some of their old functions. They were spaces where workers and passers-by could have a rest. They were refuges for the unemployed, for retired civil servants and those who wanted to escape their cramped homes for a thou-sand and one reasons. In them you could hear the clatter of backgammon and people playing cards, you could smell tea and coffee and the aromatic tobacco used in shishas. In the old days famous musicians would perform in them, singing songs with long overtures, many reprises and crooning that came from deep in the belly. Nowadays the television occupies a key corner. There are new singers you don't know who use their noses instead of their throats. They proliferate like weeds, on countless satellite channels. Alongside them gyrate young women who have been discovered you know not where, women with long legs and narrow hips, in tight trousers or short skirts, women of a kind unseen in streets where nowadays you rarely find a woman even with her head uncovered.

The football match against the Asian team ended in a 3–2 victory for the local players. The few customers in the café were watching the last minutes as you went in, and as soon as the match was over the waiter turned the television off, the noise subsided and the customers turned to conversation or playing cards. Some of them left at the end of the match, which was only available by special subscription, while others came in, apparently less enthusiastic about football.

The man sitting alone at the table opposite you didn't move. He had his back to the television and he almost sighed in relief when the match ended. He was in his late sixties. Rather sullen. A narrow wedding ring shone on his veined right hand. His hand lay splayed on top of a book but the title wasn't visible. He had large sunglasses that covered half his face and was wearing a light blue shirt and dark blue trousers. His hair was dyed. It must have been. The jet black was not convincing. The same for his thin moustache, which looked like a fine thread above his thick upper lip. The neat way he dressed suggested a middle-class man who had fallen on hard times. He definitely wasn't from the city of Sindbad, although many people from there frequented the cafés in the downtown area, continuing a tradition they had acquired at home. You saw him smile once when a fat boy with Down's syndrome came along, stopped in front of him and shook his big bottom. Clearly the fat boy was a local landmark and one of the street's distinguishing features. The assistants from the nearby shops had been harassing him playfully, asking him to shake his big bottom again, and he complied with a pleasure that was saddening. The man looked behind him. He lifted his big sunglasses off his eyes and looked at you, then at Badr. He must have heard some of your conversation, because he said, 'Sorry to bother you, but where are you from?'

'From here,' you said.

'You must live abroad,' he said.

'How did you know?'

'It shows,' he answered.

You didn't ask him how it showed that you lived abroad. How could he know the contents of your black box with just one glance at the table where you were sitting, in the same streets you walked as a young man? Again, and for a last time, the man turned his face towards you, while his body, which showed a flexibility you hadn't expected from a man of his age, remained static. 'Might we have met before?' he asked. 'I don't think so,' you replied, curtly and firmly. Perhaps it was your terse responses that made him stop interrogating you. He turned his back to you again. But when the man had raised his sunglasses the first time, and you saw his melancholy eyes, a tangled skein of memories began to roll around in your head. The threads were hard to unravel. You felt that one of the threads was about this man in particular. He was very much like Mr Shakib, who had taught language and literature at the Upright Generation Secondary School and who had noticed the devil of poetry hovering around you. But a strange feeling of indifference towards things suddenly came over you, and you stopped wondering who he was.

You told Badr that you used to sit in this café, that you began your poetic life here, amid the clatter of backgammon pieces and the cries of the waiters, that the man who had helped you take the first steps along the path of poetry was a romantic poet called Salman, who used to tell you that real poets don't live to be forty. You told Badr that at one of the tables inside the café you had read a book that had greatly changed you, and that a poet called Hamed Alwan – who had a sharp tongue that was always critical, and a loud laugh that shook the whole café when he laughed, and who was killed in a mysterious car accident – always used to sit in the centre, and that a stout adolescent with thick glasses used to carry around books that weighed more than he did and used to call out to you at the top of his voice from the other end of the street and that . . . The names you mentioned sounded strange to him, the incidents unexciting. So you shut up. You didn't tell him that when you were living in the area visible right in front of you, you had travelled to the city of Sindbad, taking a taxi through towns and villages, parched oases and checkpoints in the scorching month of August, and carried in the heel of your high boots, which were fashionable among young men at the time, a message of unknown content that you had to deliver to the founder of your secret organisation, who was living there in political asylum. Nor did you tell him that the secret message, which the man in charge of domestic operations placed in a cavity he cut out of your high-heeled boots (was it the right boot or the left?), was probably important, and that the answer, which you carried on your way back, must have been even more important. You didn't tell him, because the names, the events and the timing are all so entangled that even you yourself find it hard to put them in correct chronological sequence.

One of the three paper kites that were flying free over part of the town disappeared. You don't know what happened to it. One of the other two kites tried to swoop on the other, like a bird of prey. The man who looked like your teacher at the Upright Generation Secondary School disappeared and was replaced by a solidly built man with an enormous moustache of the kind worn by truck drivers. Your son Badr disappeared. The gold ring disappeared from the ring finger of your left hand. You heard a voice repeating, insistently and annoyingly, a name that had an unsettling resonance: Younis, Younis. You turned to where the voice came from. You saw a young man with a pale complexion, stocky, wearing thick glasses and carrying a thick book, urging you to leave. He was smoking with ostentatious voracity, as adolescents usually do. With his usual impatience, he said, 'Drink up your tea quickly. We're late for our appointment with Ghaith.'

VIII

You were embarrassed by the two strange words and by the time you found out what they meant you were already at odds with your father. It embarrassed you that children used the words to identify your area and the street junctions, saying, for example, 'At the Nakuja Abad corner', or, 'After the Nakuja Abad house', or even worse when they called you the Nakuji in jest, a nickname that sounded obscene in the local language. The words, written over the gateway to your summer house in a Persian script, made you angry. Why had your father chosen them, rather than any of the usual formulas written at the entrances to houses in the neighbourhood? Why did he make a point of embarrassing you and your brothers in front of your local friends with this gibberish?

Some of the houses in the neighbourhood had inscriptions at their gates, with words such as 'The home of Captain Hassan Rafie' or 'This is by the Grace of God', or 'God is the Light of Heaven and Earth'. But not Nakuja Abad. Nothing like that. Your father also differed from the other men in the neighbourhood by wearing a small white cotton skullcap that covered half his head, and by having a beard, which started to turn grey early and was neatly trimmed. He was tall and slim and had a cigarette permanently in the left corner of his mouth, while with his right hand he penned words that leaned against each other like dominoes, or slumped flirtatiously like women in beds of love, or craned their necks like gazelles listening for the footsteps of predators, or that were as convoluted as a labyrinth or a viper in a bunch of grapes.

Of course your problem with your father wasn't only over these two words, or other similarly incomprehensible words, or your aversion to the Thursday salons. In fact it was your choices, or to be more precise your behaviour, that caused him to seethe with a rage that, when it reached boiling point, would explode in an outburst no one would have expected from a quiet man who was almost ascetically devoted to his workshop. You especially remember three times when your father completely lost his temper. Once when the Hamiya disciplinary council punished you, along with Khalaf and Salem, for stealing papers for the secondary school exams, when your father was summoned to appear before the council. A second time when you were caught red-handed with the banned book *The State and Revolution*. And the third time when Roula's father complained to him about your relationship with his daughter . . . There was also the inauspicious moment when the attempt was made to assassinate the Grandson. But that time he didn't explode, or rather you didn't see him explode, because you weren't there. After that critical juncture in your life, you never saw your father again. You escaped abroad. But you learnt that the incident left him deeply saddened and drove him into further seclusion. Because after the incident the Hamiya leadership dispensed with his services and put him under covert surveillance, and the elite and the media lost interest in him and his works. But that probably didn't upset your father, who had never sought publicity and was devoted to his work. What upset him, and what saddened him for years, was his disappointment that you had turned out to be the opposite of him in almost everything, and the fact that you were not close by. How could he not feel that he would never see you again? You think it was this rather than anything else that pained him, because in spite of everything, although you contested his religion, his authority and his taste in poetry, you know your father loved you. In fact, he loved in you your spirit of rebellion and inquiry and feared for the consequences it would have for you. You can be sure he reserved a special dash of paternal affection just for you. You don't know exactly why; perhaps because you were the only child who argued with him and challenged him, while your brothers obeyed him or were in awe of his prestige.

After you escaped, you and your father did correspond sporadically. Perhaps because the postal authorities were monitoring the letters, he never mentioned the Grandson incident or any of your radical disagreements: your hard-left politics, your writing of modern poetry instead of classical poems in the traditional format, which he said was essential to any proper poetry, the way you ridiculed religious beliefs, and so on. Instead he would tell you what was news at home and in the family and with relatives: who had married, who had died, what appliances or furniture had been added to the house, sometimes about a book he had read or an idea he was working on. Because of his emotionally reserved nature and his allusive style, you had to infer by interpretation and reading between the lines that he missed you, or was disappointed in you, or that you had left a void in the house. Being near or distant was a metaphysical matter, as far as your father was concerned, or that's what you concluded from what he said and from the quotations he would copy out. You thought about that at length after, in one of his letters, he quoted a fragment written by, you think, the tenth-century Sufi mystic al-Niffari. He began his letter by writing about your brother Sanad's plan to go to the Land of Palm Trees and Oil, before suddenly breaking off and writing a line across the middle of the page with a broader stroke (he clearly used one of his brushes and not a normal ink pen): 'Farness is made known by nearness, and nearness is made known by spiritual existence.' Then he went back to talking about your brother, who wanted to try his luck working and living in that country, to which some Hamiya people had started to rush after torrents of oil gushed out there.

Although metaphor was not unfamiliar in your life and your writing, your father baffled you with such fragments, which would spring from the unknown into letters that were meant to convey greetings and small talk. This was one of your problems with him: having to reinterpret a saying or a story that may not have had a meaning, in your opinion, other than the obvious one. You usually failed to relate to his metaphors or the subtext of his words, not because of some mental deficiency, as you sometimes thought, or because you are hostile to metaphors, but because you believed that reality was the proper reference point for testing words and things; that facts have an aspect that must be seen and touched, and that humanity's heaven and hell are on this earth, not in some other place. Because oppression, exploitation, injustice, and the monopolisation of power and wealth are man-made creations, and mankind will give them up only at the end of a struggle that should not hesitate to use force if necessary: violence to counter violence in order to set up a human paradise on earth. The flower is here, so let's dance here. That's what you also learned from your secret organisation's literature, and what you blindly believed.

Later, when you became less rigid in your ideas and doubts started to impinge, you read about a calligrapher who went into ecstasies and had visions – a description that reminded you somewhat of your father. The writer described the calligrapher as writing in three types of script: the first he alone could read, the second he and others could read, while neither he nor anyone else could read the third. By that time you had discovered the meaning of the two words your father had inscribed on the arched gateway of your summer house. It wasn't he who told you what they meant; you had read a chapter on Suhrawardi, the mystic who was executed, in a book devoted to troubled personalities. Suhrawardi apparently coined a Persian phrase with the meaning 'nowhere place' or 'nowhere country' – Nakuja Abad.

In *The Chant of the Wing of Gabriel*, a book by Suhrawardi, the observer asks the sage where he comes from. The sage points to his brothers, who are lined up among those who had arrived before him, and says, 'We come to you from Nakuja Abad.'

This strange linguistic coinage also made you think of *The City of Where*, the title of a renowned book by a poet from the city of Sindbad who, like his ancient forebears, crossed tame seas and dark seas, and went missing on the steppes of distant continents.

The truth is that your room had not been turned into a guest room after you left, as you wrote, even if your family did sometimes use it to put up passing guests. Such guests became fewer and fewer and eventually stopped coming with the passage of time. Your relics were still there: your books that filled a corner to one side, your bachelor's degree certificate hanging in a glass frame, a photograph of you with Khalaf and Salem in khaki clothes and wide-brimmed hats, holding terrified rabbits on a hunting trip (there was another person of your age at the edge of the picture, who might have been Wahid), a transistor radio the size of a large hand with a dark-blue leather cover that had withstood the ravages of time, an oak desk with a silver rack in the middle, holding letters and identity documents between two semicircular plates of glass. Next to it stood an empty glass vase with a lotus flower design and on the base some faint writing that probably indicated where it was made.

You no longer know how or why you acquired most of the books and you were surprised at the names of some of the authors, which you might as well never have heard of. Apart from pulling *A Prophet Who Shares My Apartment With Me* out from among the books, you didn't go near your other things. You left them staring at you, confronting you like the contents of an abandoned museum.

You were like someone postponing an inevitable confrontation for a later occasion.

In addition to the woollen mattress your mother had upholstered for you with her own hands, which had since turned to dust, there were three mattresses lying along the sides of the room. On your first night back you slept on the mattress that was printed with red anemones in an endlessly repeating pattern. You slept as you had never slept before. You forgot to take one of the sleeping pills you usually take before going to bed, which nonetheless do not always ward off the nightly visitations of insomnia. You slept without a sleeping pill. You slept long, without coughing, without dreams to disturb or comfort you, until mid-morning, when you were invaded in your bed by the sound of the children and the smell of coffee. You washed your face and brushed your teeth. You combed what's left of your hair. You went to the big kitchen your father designed for the family to gather at meal-times, so that the women of the family could chat and discuss domestic matters and your brothers could take refuge from receiving your father's unexpected guests. It's both a kitchen and a family room, with one corner spread with carpets and cushions on the ground and one corner with a dining table and chairs that are rarely used. The whole family was waiting for you in the kitchen, except your brother Sanad, who lives with his family in the Land of Palm Trees and Oil. The brothers and sisters who were children when you escaped now had wives and husbands, sons and daughters so numerous and so close in age that it was hard for you to remember their faces and their names. Your brother Shihab, the third male born to your mother's fertile womb, has named his second son Younis. That was a courtesy that greatly touched you. That was your first morning in the house and among family members, and it was filled with familiar images and smells after an absence that had lasted twenty years.

Younis hovered around you, nine or ten years old with round eyes. He showed you something in the kitchen cupboards, named the plants and the house things as if he were renaming the species that had survived the great flood. 'This is snapdragon,' he told you. 'This is basil. This is gera-nium. This is my grandmother's prayer rug. That's my grand-father's favourite cup. These are eggplants. This is ghee. Do you like ghee, Uncle?'

After taking you on a verbal tour of the things in the house, he said, 'It's better here, right?'

You stroked his short-cropped hair, which reminded you of your own hair when you were his age, and smiled at him. In return he gave you a bigger smile.

The real reception room, or what you call the diwan, hasn't changed. It's on the ground floor, right next to the front door of the house. It's a traditional architectural layout, meant to keep the guests, especially outsiders, away from the interior of the house and from the intimate spaces reserved for the family and their closest relatives.

The members of your family use all the floors and most of the rooms in the house, which is built of black volcanic stone (except for the arched gateway which is made of dusty white stone), but the diwan, which is rectangular, seems to have preserved the smells and spectres of the past. As though it hasn't been used for ages. After your father died, it was no longer the venue for the Thursday salons that witnessed lengthy discussions about Ibn Muqla the Abbasid vizier and his pioneering work in the field of calligraphy, the additional contributions of Ishaq Ibn al-Nadim, the innovations of Ibn al-Bawwab, and the contemporary work of Hamid al-Amadi and al-Dirani. The participants would bandy about the names of calligraphers, Sufis and poets, ancient and modern, questioning or casting doubt on what others were saying. Your father's knowing words would modestly decide the matter, because he was the arbiter and ultimate authority among his friends, especially on questions of calligraphy and Sufism, which in his case arose from both a passion and a deep inner commitment, and meant more than merely repeating dry rules and metaphysical abstractions. They didn't talk only about calligraphers and the various ways they made their letters twist and turn, stretch and double back. They might also talk about the heresy trial of Ibn Hanbal and the crucifixion of al-Hallaj, the murder of Suhrawardi and Ibn Arabi's views on the unity of existence, al-Niffari's books *The Stations* and *The Addresses*, and then jump centuries forward to Taha Hussein and his scepticism about pre-Islamic poetry and the argument about his controversial ideas. (Apart from Taha Hussein, you didn't know most of these names.) Sometimes your father would force you to attend these Thursday salons and you would hover between boredom and drowsiness among men who seemed to you to have just emerged from the Middle Ages. The subjects he discussed with his friends did not interest you, the names they mentioned were not familiar and the music they listened to and nodded their heads to, either in rapture or absent-mindedly, left you quite cold, especially the music in which the lines were repeated again and again, turning on themselves, like whirling dervishes, with irritating monotony. Your father's Thursday salons, which you were forced to attend in the long summer holidays, were like torture sessions for your restless body and for your spirit, which was adrift in a domain very far from their own world with its clouds of dust from the golden ages. You would rather play with your friends, fight in the back streets, sharpen knives, chase everything that moved on the face of the earth or, when you grew older, go to cafés and meet poets and young writers who were interested, like you, in modern literature.

Young Younis was walking beside you like an undersized shadow when you went into the diwan. You saw the sofas, the chairs and the wooden coffee-tables, some of them inlaid with mother-of-pearl. The room evoked old voices, the smells of coffee with cardamom, lemonade with rose water and incense brought from distant climes. Your father's calligraphies were still staring down from the walls, some words legible and others illegible.

You remembered that you very much liked one of his works in particular; it was a design that bore the last half of a line of verse and read: *Souls yearn for you for eternity*. Your father had written it in the *thuluth* style, which was one of his favourites and in which he designed notable masterpieces.

His books were still in the wooden bookcase, looking down on you with their spines of gilt leather. The only new thing in the diwan was a black-and-white picture of him, taken by the Grandson's private photographer, showing him in his workshop, engrossed in writing a large inscription in Kufic script.

When young Younis saw you looking at the picture, he said, 'That's your father, right?'

'That's right,' you said.

'You're Younis, and I'm Younis, right?'

'That's right, and there's a third one too, apart from us,' you said.

'Where's he?' he said.

'It's hard to see him,' you said.

'He's a ghost, you mean?'

'Maybe.'

With his round eyes, young Younis looked at the photograph and said, 'My father put it here. It used to be downstairs.'

You know this picture well. It never used to hang in the diwan but, as young Younis said, in the workshop that took up the cellar of the summer house. Your father was wearing a khaki shirt and trousers, which were common in Hamiya, in fact the standard work clothes there. The military differed from the others in that they had ranks and regimental badges, but not in the colour of their clothes. Your father wasn't a military man but at work he used to wear this uniform, without badges to show his rank or the service he belonged to. He wasn't looking at the photographer, in fact he didn't even seem to be aware of his presence. His right hand was holding a wooden pencil. His head and body were bent over, his eyes looking at the spot where the pencil rested on the sheet of paper. His shoulders were thin and hunched and slightly tense. Fragile, engrossed in his letters, he seemed to be in a trance. You could see the Kufic writing, as intricate as a maze, but it was hard to read it in the picture.

Your father wrote few words in his designs. Despite his devoutness, he wasn't inclined to use Quranic verses, common sayings of the Prophet or long sentences. Some of his designs consisted of a single letter, such as *nun, ba, kaf* or *alif*, with a little decoration such as foliage in the empty spaces. Even with the ancient poems that he loved, many of which he knew by heart, he seldom put a whole line in one of his designs. Maybe he wanted to leave it to the eye of the beholder to wander in the void. As if to be incomplete was the way things really were. *Kullu man alayhi faanin*, 'Everyone upon it is ephemeral', one of them read. You hadn't known how to read this early design of your father's. Especially the word *faanin*, 'ephemeral'. It wasn't until you grew up that you realised it was connected with the word *fanaa*, 'transcendence'. You remember that he refused to write in full that famous line of Mutanabbi's, starting *To the extent that people are resolute*, when he wrote the inscription on the triumphal arch at the entrance to Hamiya.

In the face of opposition from the Grandson's aides, he broke the inscription off after the first seven words. If it had been his choice, he would not have written even those words, which he considered, as far as you remember from a discussion that took place in the Thursday salon, to be pretentious and boastful, a sycophantic suggestion by the Grandson's retinue. You were surprised how little decoration and foliage there was in the calligraphies that hung on the walls of the diwan. Apparently the empty space that calligraphers avoid, either for fear of a void or because they lack ingenuity, did not frighten your father. In fact the empty space so evident in some of his works may have been quite deliberate. It had a presence that was clear and unsettling at the same time. You had seen most of these designs before but you had never thought about this aspect. During your long absence and in your wanderings through numerous countries you had seen the work of many calligraphers, most of whom resort to decorative foliage and filling in the background of the design or the inscription itself in a way that diverts the eye. You don't recall many of your father's opinions on the art of calligraphy, but you imagine he would have seen excessive decoration as aesthetic padding that distracted from contemplation of the secret hidden in the letter or the word. Calligraphy in its absolute union with the letter and the word, which were united in their turn in a higher secret, was what mattered to him, and besides that, manual craftsmanship. Perhaps that explains why your father preferred to be called a calligrapher rather than an artist. Maybe he saw in art a creativity and playfulness that he did not believe in. Creation was for God. As for playing with letters and words that had conveyed countless inexhaustible connotations over hundreds of years, by his standards that was an adolescent folly that humanity had not grown out of. Such talk might have been aimed at you. His criticism of you was along these lines and you knew this, and you would answer him in the same manner. But playing with words that say one thing and mean something else delighted your father and encouraged him to bring the best of them out of his lexical treasure trove. You were his favourite partner in this chess game of words and meaning.

It was young Younis who took you down to the cellar where your father had spent long hours in summer mixing inks, sharpening pencils, boiling tea, rubbing pieces of paper with organic substances or writing, often with a single stroke of his pen, a large letter in a design he was working on. Breathing fitfully, you went down the twelve steps that you knew by heart. Young Younis had gone ahead and was waiting for you at the cellar door. He stood upright and stuck out his chest, with his firm hands locked behind his back, like a soldier on parade.

Like the diwan, the cellar had been left as it was, as if your father, wearing his khaki shirt and trousers, might come in at any moment, after taking off his snow-white gown and his embroidered black cloak in his bedroom, keeping only his white skullcap on. You felt that strongly. You could almost hear his breathing as he came down the twelve steps to the cellar. You could smell the faint scent of musk, the smell of his trimmed beard after Friday prayers. There were several designs, complete or incomplete, on the cellar walls, on the work-bench and on the bookshelves. On the edge of the workbench there was a round ashtray made of brass and engraved with five-petalled flowers, with four grooves around the rim to hold cigarettes, and a dark green patch in the base.

You noticed that under the bench there was a pair of green plastic slippers that he apparently used when he was washing before prayers or when moving around the cellar. You took off your sandals and put the slippers on. They were your size. You remembered that you, your father and your brother Sanad all took the same size: 43. You remembered your brother, who had moved to the Land of Palm Trees and Oil. You used to filch his favourite shoes when the male hormones started to kick in. He would go crazy when he had an appointment and couldn't find his shoes. He knew you had got to them first and he would have to change his trousers to match the colour of the only other shoes that were available.

While you gazed around at your father's workshop, at his tools and his relics, young Younis was standing upright, his hands behind his back, in front of a large design in Kufic script in a corner near the entrance to the cellar. It was the same design that could be seen in the photograph hanging in the diwan. Framed in a perfect square, it was severely geometric and appeared to be formed of pixels, as in today's digital images.

You had seen the design before but hadn't noticed the maze, in which he had tried out two gradations of turquoise. You thought it was just a geometrical game. Your father, who did not usually play with calligraphy, wanted to play, to try out the surprising possibilities that playing would reveal, or to combine calligraphy and the graphic design for which he faulted your brother Sanad. He was not one of those who used Kufic much, but even when he did it wasn't in this geometric style that looked as though it were computer-generated. The precision with which your father had executed his Kufic design was amazing. It was in the form of a maze, but a geometric maze based on the uprights and right angles of the letters. Young Younis, who turned towards you when he sensed you standing behind him, knew something you did not know, or had not paid any attention to. With his firm little hand he pointed towards the picture and said, 'Can you read it?' His question took you by surprise. Can I in fact read it, you wondered. The way the letters were interlocked, in a starkly geometrical structure, made it difficult if not impossible, and you repeated the same question to him. 'Can you read it?' you joked (were you really joking?). 'I can,' he said. 'Very well, read it,' you said. 'Lift me up,' he said. You hesitated a moment. You were just about to have a coughing fit, but you held it back. You brought your father's chair from behind his desk. Young Younis stood on it. He pointed his little hand to an empty space between two blocks of writing in the upper middle of the design and said, 'That's where we go in.' Then to an empty space on the left-hand side and said, 'And that's where we come out.' 'Clear enough,' I told my nephew. 'That's the way in and that's the way out, but you haven't read what's written.' 'Look,' he said. 'Where we go in it's the word *diiq* and we come out at *faraj*, and the longest path between the entrance and the exit is through the word *hayra*. Do you know what *hayra* means, Uncle?' 'I know,' I said.

What young Younis said threw light on mysterious aspects of your father's design. The words and lines emerged from a state of occultation to one of epiphany, as the Sufis say, and what you thought was playing really was playing, but playing by someone who, in an intricate and abstruse manner, was writing the elements of some redemptive talisman. The starting point of the design was the word *diiq*, 'anguish'. You managed to work out the interlocking letters after young Younis pronounced them. The end point was the word *faraj*, 'relief'. Then the word *hayra*, 'uncertainty'. But in the middle was a fourth word that young Younis didn't say, a word that offered a shorter way out of the maze. You made out the letter *sin* and then the *a* at the end of the word. The two dots were next to the *a*, not on top of it. Then you saw an open rectangle with another identical rectangle right underneath it. It was the letter *kaf*. Then it was clear to you that the fourth word, which offered a shorter way out of the maze, was *sakiina*, 'peace of mind'.

IX

You told your relatives you didn't want the whole world to know you were back. Your brother Shihab, now the head of the family, objected and said that custom required throwing a party to celebrate your return. You rejected the idea with a vehemence that hurt his feelings. Then you tried to ease the situation by saying you were exhausted from the journey and uneasy after so many years away, and you wanted to rest among them a while before they held the party, to which you would invite those closest to you and your old friends that remained. You calmed things down with this compromise, which postponed the challenge of meeting people you no longer knew and to whom you did not have much to say. But this wish of yours was not entirely honoured. You deduced this from the fact that certain people started passing in front of your house, people who hadn't passed by very often since you escaped, since your brother Sanad went away and your father died. That's what young Younis told you, reporting a conversation between his father and mother. So one of them had leaked the news of your return.

Sitting in the diwan, you told your brother Shihab that the news of your arrival was no longer a secret and apparently there were people who had heard. Shihab, who seemed emotionally cold on the outside, said that no such thing had happened. Someone might have seen you and recognised you when you went to visit your parents' graves. Then he said it didn't matter because people were no longer as you had known them, and you were mistaken if you thought that the bonds between people here did not break in the same way as anywhere else. But what you heard from young Younis was true, or that's what the remains of your vanity led you to believe. On the third or fourth day after your return, from the balcony that overlooks Muntazah Street, you saw Roula walking along bolt upright, wearing a black dress that reached to below the knee, with two children beside her and a third jaunting along behind her. Your heart beat so hard you thought they must have heard it throughout the house. In the pit of your lungs you felt a coughing fit coming on. You held it down with the palm of your hand. None of the adults were near by. There was young Younis telling you about his school and his knowledge of foreign literature, while you were watching the sun slowly set on a horizon flecked with red. When Roula was level with your house she looked up at the balcony. She saw you. But you don't know whether she recognised you because she shielded her eyes with her right hand against the remaining rays of a sun that was still strong. Young Younis was reciting a famous foreign poem that compares life to a stage. You interrupted him and said, 'Do you see that woman?' You pointed at her. You told him, 'Go and call her. Tell her your mother wants to see her urgently.' Young Younis shot off like an arrow across the large balcony on the third floor and down the side stairs. He disappeared and then reappeared in front of the arched gateway. Then you saw him in the street. He seemed to be calling Roula, because she stopped. Then you saw them talking and young Younis's hand pointing to the house, not to the balcony where a middle-aged tiger lay in ambush for her with his memories. You went down to the kitchen on the second floor of the house. You called your brother Shihab, who was there with his wife and some of your sisters, smoking almost non-stop, imitating your father in the way he left his cigarette burning in the left corner of his mouth. You took him aside and told him what had happened. You told him, 'It happened suddenly, so now try to find a solution.' You went to your room. You changed the pyjamas you were wearing for a shirt and trousers. You stood in front of the mirror. You combed your hair quickly. You put some light cologne on your face, similar to the 555 brand that was popular before you escaped. In front of the mirror your nervousness was obvious. Your face showed signs of two conflicting emotions, each one pulling in a different direction, as though two separate epochs were trying to dictate their terms to you. You didn't notice that your right eyelash twitched several times. You weren't aware that your hand, which was still holding the comb, was shaking. You put the comb on the dressing table and it made a sound as if it had fallen from a height. You opened your bag, where most of your clothes remained, not yet hung on hangers. From a plastic container for medicines, you took out a packet. You opened it and swallowed a tablet. You felt the tablet slide slowly down your throat. You went back to the mirror. You stood stock still in front of it. Did you want to make sure you looked right for the occasion? Or to see the map that the years, your travels, trials and tribulations had etched on your face? Whatever the reason, you said to yourself, 'I'm not the only one who's changed, whose hair has turned grey, who has wrinkles starting to spread across his face, who has puffy bags under his eyes. I'm not the only one who's been battered by fate, whose tattered sails have been blown to distant shores by winds and storms. I'm not alone. I'm not alone. She must have changed too, because from the balcony she looked like her picture in the newspaper when she received the Medal of Duty from the Grandson.' Apparently you hadn't been standing in front of the mirror for long when young Younis burst into the room, panting.

She was in the third year of middle school when you first saw her. Before that, just like other adolescents whose bodies had been shaken by new and unfamiliar impulses, you, Salem and Khalaf used to pursue a local girl, the daughter of the woman who owned the Mothers grocery, a girl who was susceptible to pursuit because her school was conveniently remote. Your heart was liable to throb audibly inside your ribs and you had little control over what went on between your legs. You also especially remember Widad, the girl next door, and the cream nightdress that clung to her body when she was washing the veranda of their house. The girl who smelled of perfumed soap. It almost came back to you now, the same arousal you felt when you saw the roundness of her firm bottom and the way she looked back, half embarrassed and half in collusion, when she saw your mouth agape, looking at her bottom and at the black underwear that showed through the wet night-dress. But until you saw Roula all these pursuits and early arousals had nothing to do with what you had heard and read about love.

You were borrowing a book from the public library when your eyes fell on Roula, the girl to whom you would later say, 'Your hair is like a flock of goats descending from Mount

Gilead'; the girl to whom you would write, loosely inspired by the Song of Solomon, 'I remember the smell of your mouth better than the taste of wine, your underarm better than the smell of apple,' even before you had tasted wine and before the sweetness of her mouth had become a memory; the girl who would write to you on pink notepaper after she discovered the source of your pastoral poetry and you began to share its gifts in secret: 'Sustain me with cakes of raisins, refresh me with apples, for I am lovesick.' You didn't know the key to attracting women. You thought it was strength. Acting tough. Combing your hair with a quiff. It didn't occur to you that words might be more powerful, when allied with inspiration. It was Roula who made you believe that you possessed, in words, a dangerous weapon you would use often after that, sometimes honestly, sometimes dishonestly, sometimes with success, sometimes without. With two of her colleagues, who looked like ladies-in-waiting, Roula was borrowing some reference book from the library. One of Hamiya's virtues was that it encouraged students to research scientific subjects and the classics and to be competitive, so it provided a large public library for this purpose. You couldn't keep your eyes off her eyes. She had big dark eyes, very black and very white, that stared perpetually into an unknown the depth of which was hard to gauge. She had two deadly dimples, especially when she smiled or laughed. She had a mouth like the bud of a Persian rose flecked with the dewdrops of a northern dawn, or so you thought, though you had never heard of or seen such a flower. As with the epiphanies of which the Sufis talk, or the inspirations that descend on poets from angels or devils, you knew she was the one your restless soul was seeking. At that moment you surrendered voluntarily to the power of those eyes, the dimples, the hair that trailed down like a flock of goats on Mount Gilead. You left the library before her. You waited an age for her. You didn't know what you would say, what you would do with your stray hands. On other occasions you had had casual flirtatious words ready in your head and you had control over your hands. This time you succumbed to a state of lightness, weightlessness, imminent flight, and one phrase, or to be precise one feeling, took control of you. When she came out between her two ladies-in-waiting, you looked straight at her, ignoring the presence of the other two, who might as well have disappeared. With your legs trembling, your hands waving aimlessly, your tongue tangled, you said, 'Excuse me.' 'Sorry?' she replied. 'Excuse me,' you repeated. Her dimples played like the eyes of a storm about to break, and she said, 'Excuse me what?' 'I want to have a word with you,' you said. You can't remember whether her friends stayed close by or moved away. You can't remember, because you couldn't see anything but her. It was she who stepped forward to where you were standing at the entrance to the library. Several steps to the right, where a giant cinchona tree cast a mammoth shadow on the ground. You seemed to be luring her in. You weren't of course. Perhaps you stepped back because of the simple phrase that imposed itself upon you. Right under the cinchona tree, with the eyes of that storm about to break in her dimples, she stopped. She didn't show any sign that she knew what you were about to say (or so it seemed to you). 'Yes?' she said. 'I love you,' you said. 'What?' she asked, and the eyes of the storm played again on her cheeks. 'I love you,' you said firmly. 'Are you mad?' she said. 'Not always!' you replied.

You didn't know who she was. Unlike her. Because she had seen you before. She had heard of what she called your escapades, such as the incident when you stole the exam questions, and then the branding incident, which was fresh at the time and common knowledge among young people. In Hamiya such news didn't need legs or a megaphone.

Although Hamiya is divided into separate encampments, one for each branch of the armed forces, each with its own housing complex and facilities including schools, there are meeting points that bring people together, such as the traditional central market, the park that is famous for its cinchona trees, the domed library, the sports stadium and the gyms, the art galleries and the cinemas. So people with common interests can meet up. In one of these places Roula had seen you before. After meeting her in the public library, you found out that she was the daughter of the commander of the Grandson's palace guard. But you weren't interested in her father's sensitive position. You were not a complete unknown. You had the makings of a promising poet, as Hamiya's weekly newspaper put it when it commented on a poem it had published at just that time, and you were also the son of the Calligrapher. In fact these considerations never occurred to you. You were living as though you had wings, living dreams that hovered above the harshness of reality, living life with a boldness that looked like recklessness to many. That's what mattered to you. That and nothing else. Despite your attempts to be discreet and secretive in your meetings with Roula 'out of respect' for her father, as she put it, the story of your love affair soon leaked out and drove her father to complain to your father. Your father, who was in no way held to blame, was furious. His anger had no effect on you. You had been swept far away, on a powerful wave of emotion you had not known before. But Roula started to discover in you things she didn't like, or things she hoped to avoid so that your love might have a happy ending, such as your tendency to make hasty judgments, the banned books you were reading, your pointed criticism of the Hamiya leadership, your lack of respect for your elders and for convention. 'Respect for elders' was the precise expression she used in one of your angry discussions. The traditional ring of it, coming from a girl of sixteen, almost made you crack up laughing. But with a hug, or with one of your surprising turns of phrase, you could make her forget the subject in dispute and set her dimples back to work. She loved your explanation of her name. The second or third time you met, you told her, 'The Roula are Arabs whose palaces are tents.' But she didn't understand. She thought you were making fun of her name. You told her that it came from the first half of a line of poetry that included her name, perhaps the only Arabic reference available for the name. She asked you what the line of poetry meant, and you said it was about some Arabs who bore her name, a tribe that is, whose palaces were tents. But she preferred the other meaning you came up with at another meeting. You had searched through all the encyclopaedias in the Hamiya library, and you came across the theory that the name Roula was a corruption of a Latin word meaning 'lady of the city'. After that you started calling her 'lady of the city'. She liked that, especially when you told her about how, when you first saw her, you imagined her companions as ladies-in-waiting to a princess from another world. She tried to defend her friends, saying they were dear friends and not ladies-in-waiting to her or anyone else, but that didn't prevent a sly narcissistic glitter showing in her eyes.

The name 'lady of the city' spread among the young people of Hamiya after you had a poem published with that title, a poem that imitated the Song of Solomon because you were enthralled by its pastoral lyricism and its ingenuity in describing love. The local teenagers liked the poem so much that a new boutique selling women's fashions called itself Lady of the City. But the story of your love, which reached her father, was about to run up against an event that was taking shape in the womb of the unknown, an event that would have repercussions you did not expect.

There were several secret organisations that were active. Some of them concentrated on trying to assassinate the Grandson, without notable success, while others tried to bring about a popular revolution and organise civil disobedience campaigns, but they didn't succeed either, because the situation in the country was stable, security was under control thanks to the hidden forces keeping watch, and living conditions were reasonable for most people, perhaps better than elsewhere in your troubled part of the world. Why should they rise up against the Grandson and the status quo? For freedom? To express themselves? For democracy? To take part in government? These were imported ideas, according to the phrase favoured in the local press and media. The men of religion urged the common people to obey their rulers. It was a religious duty prescribed in the Book. That's what they preached at Friday prayers and on feast days, when the Grandson made sure he was in the front row in his brocade gown with his ruddy face. But that didn't stop the formation of secret associations that were hostile to the establishment and vented their wrath at the Grandson and his corrupt coterie, as they liked to put it. In one of the many attempts to assassinate the Grandson, the commander of his guards was killed: Roula's father. It happened a year or more after you met her. The standard of living of Roula's family didn't change after the head of the family was assassinated, because the Grandson maintained all her father's privileges just as they were while he was alive, as well as awarding him the new honorary status of an officer who had fallen in the line of duty. The death of her father was an earthquake that traumatised Roula. Her attachment to her father was unequalled. The first unfortunate repercussion of his assassination on your relationship was that she held you indirectly responsible for what had happened. She didn't hold you personally responsible, but she said that the 'poisonous ideas' that you parroted were responsible for the murder of her father ('parroted' was precisely the word she used, which was insulting to your youthful pride). At the time you weren't yet involved in any organised activity, and the organisation you would later join was not the one that made the failed attempt to assassinate the Grandson. It was another, similar organisation that thought in the same way and repeated similar slogans. But one of the good repercussions of her father's death (if one may use such an inappropriate expression) was that you started to meet more often, and almost overtly. In fact, maybe it was that horrific event which paved the way for what would follow. Khalaf was close to your relationship. You happened to meet in his presence several times, or you would entrust your friend who hated books with the task of conveying messages to her because you were busy with something else. By that time you had joined a secret organisation that was called To Work, not because a book with a similar name was part of its ideological literature, but because it believed in deeds rather than words.

Theorising did not play a prominent role in the culture of your organisation. In that respect it made do with a few books and leaflets printed abroad and smuggled to you in complicated ways. These were your inexhaustible and unquestionable gospels, the teachings of the prophets of revolution with their thick grey beards and their long hair.

Theorising, in the opinion of your leaders, was a game, a pastime for the petty bourgeoisie, just like 'joining the ranks of the masses', the policy pursued by the largest organisation in the arena. Your organisation was not against the masses; in fact it insisted on speaking in their name, but it believed that an organised elite could bring about change and 'skip stages' rather than wait for objective circumstances to mature. In your opinion revolutionary violence was necessary to push forward the creaky wheel of history.

How long did your relationship last? Not long compared with all the water that has since flowed under the bridge. Less than four years. From the moment you told her 'I love you' without prior warning, to the moment when you promised her you would be reunited as soon as possible. You were telling her the truth, because you were in love and could not bear to be apart, and also because all you could see at the time was the moment and your immediate surroundings. Because how could you have known, when you promised to stay close to her, that your exile would last twenty years and that the fates conspiring in the heart of future time would send winds to carry your sail further and further away, right to the edge of the dark waters? But the affairs of the heart, and maybe of memory, are not measured in days. They have another scale that you don't quite know. So her image kept pursuing you. If it ever slipped your mind, it would soon reappear. At least in the first years of your journey. Every female face you saw, every gait, every glance, every voice, every hand gesture, every dress and shawl and pair of shoes and pair of underwear, every bottle of perfume, powder compact and stick of lipstick you automatically compared with her face, her gait, the way she turned her head, her husky voice, the way she moved her hands, her dresses and shawls and underwear, her perfumes and make-up. Even the smells revealed only in moments of passionate physical contact were pleasant or repellent to the extent that they were similar to or different from the smells of her naked body. They were the references that found a home in your memory and laid a foundation for love and desire. The references that became a benchmark, that started to operate, by a mechanism of their own and independently of your consciousness, with every woman with whom you later had a relationship. Even after you married the woman you met on the Island of the Sun. When you kiss a woman you want to taste the wild honey of the first saliva you tasted. When you embrace you want to put your hand around that waist you used to encircle with just one hand. When you move close to her neck you want to detect the faint smell of sweat and jasmine combined. When you put your hand on her breasts, you want to feel them tremble like a brace of trapped partridges. When you lick her navel it has to reveal childhood secrets. When you go even lower, you expect the smell of marjoram. When you enter her, you prepare yourself, midway, for the pulsations and contractions of *her* vagina, for the way *she* held her breath as though she were about to die. You don't know why these images, these smells and tactile sensations have been filed away so carefully in your head. You don't know if they were so divine, so exciting and normative at the time. But that's how they became. Your marriage to the Island of the Sun woman was not just a matter of solidarity in the struggle and admiration for her experience and what she said. There was also emotion and desire. Admiration and desire for a body. But why, whenever you slept with her, did you imagine you were sleeping with the woman whose vulva smelled of marjoram and basil and freshly crushed wheat? Was it the influence of the Song of Solomon? But no, words have no smells or textures unless they have some reference in one's memory. Why was I enthralled by the ordinary in Roula and thought it such a wonder: her fingers, her feet, her neck, the many freckles on her shoulder blades, the way she opened her mouth and smiled, her husky voice, the expressive power of her dimples? Her shawl when it slipped off her shoulder. Her dress riding above her knees when she sat down. Her tense thumbs slowly removing her underwear. The repeated kisses after making love, lying skin to skin before you fell asleep together, while you slept and after you slept. What disturbed you most were the kisses that followed making love with any other woman; you usually did that out of a sense of duty or courtesy. Complete fusion, the melding of bodies and beyond bodies, getting under the skin: that happened only with Roula. Was it complete emotional and physical fulfilment? Or does the extraordinary power of nostalgia exaggerate what was minor and erase the margins, the peripheral, the accompanying symptoms, while preserving the stable essence, an elixir that might be of nostalgia's own making, impervious to the ravages of time? Nostalgia, that disease or form of ignorance, to use the expression of a writer who examined it in its many elusive guises and did not come to any clear conclusion. You have suffered that disease. Here's an amusing practical example. You love mint tea. Everywhere you have lived there was tea, but there wasn't always mint, especially in the City of Red and Grey. But nonetheless you would contrive to obtain a sprig of mint, stealing it from parks that cultivate herbs and plants that come from hot countries as well as cold. You would make tea your mother's way: pour bottled mineral water into a teapot (because tap water is too hard). Put some sugar in, at least a cup of sugar when the water starts to warm up. Before it boils, throw a handful of loose tea into the pot. Bring everything to the boil. Turn the stove off. Lift the lid and put the sprig of mint in. Leave the tea to brew a while. Put the pot on a tray next to an empty glass. Take the tray close to the window where your desk is. Sit behind the desk. Light a cigarette. Pour the tea into the empty glass. Sip it once, twice. Take a puff of your cigarette. But the mint tea that you've prepared, although you've made it properly, doesn't match the tea of your memory.

Young Younis didn't budge from the room. He just said, 'They're waiting for you in the diwan.' He remained standing a few feet away from you. You remembered your first meeting with Roula, the words 'I love you' and how, as her dimples prepared to make a storm, she said, 'Are you mad?' The smell of the cinchona trees, the kisses, the letters that came close to the Song of Solomon, the perfumed lock of hair, morning coffees in the central market, the suns that rose and the suns that set, the storms, the biting cold, Khalaf's face and his eyes avoiding you. A videotape with a thousand and one images, replayed at speed as you looked inanely in the mirror.

Suddenly, something happened that you hadn't expected.

You felt that all your sensations – the rise and fall of your breathing, your heartbeat, fast or slow, all the images that passed one by one through your head – were happening to someone else you could see in the mirror. You could feel exactly what he felt, and see the images, fast and slow, that went through his mind, but he wasn't you. It was as if the two of you had been one person and then you had quietly split in two, like space ships undocking on a television screen. But you were strongly aware of him nonetheless. You even felt that his mouth was dry and he was trying to moisten it by producing a little saliva. There were three of you in the room: you, the other person in the mirror and young Younis, whose round eyes were darting between you and the mirror. You thought it had happened under the influence of the tranquilliser you had just taken. But no. Because when you put your hand on the shoulder of young Younis and said, 'Let's go', the hand of the man looking out at you from the mirror did not move. He kept staring at you with looks that ranged between pity and expectation.

With her hair tied back and her black dress raised to her knees, Roula was sitting on a chair under the calligraphy that read *Souls yearn for you for eternity*. You told yourself it might have been a coincidence, though to you she retained some of that aura of princess she had in distant days. She too liked that poem, which you had read to her. Your brother Shihab and his wife Fadwa were talking to her. You heard her voice before you went into the diwan, saying that she had been going to the park for a walk. It was the same slightly husky voice. The huskiness that used to make your head spin. Then you heard Fadwa say that you had been shutting yourself up in the room all the time. Then you went into the diwan. She stood up and greeted you. She looked shorter than you remembered her. 'Welcome back,' she said. 'Thank you,' you replied. 'It's been a long absence,' she said. 'Indeed!' you said.

Then she asked, 'Just visiting or back for good?' 'I'm not sure yet,' you said. Her dimples were in action, both when she was speaking and when she was listening. You felt that they were about to take off with full force but they didn't. Some kind of intentional self-control held them back. The two of you didn't know where to begin. All the things you said at the start were laborious attempts to discover the path the conversation should take. You didn't come across that path. The conversation remained desultory. It went back and forth but didn't lock on to a particular track. It was the talk of strangers, or of people who last met a long time ago. So commonplace talk was safer. She asked you if you found the country changed. 'Sure,' you said. 'Everything's changed,' she said, 'even the weather.' Then she fell silent. You found yourself telling her, 'That's the case everywhere. Places change and people too.' You chatted a little about how change was the way of the world, and then you shut up. She said you had become famous, and you said, 'Not very. It's actors and singers who can be described as famous, not writers. At least, not writers like me.' She said, 'But we've seen your picture in the papers several times.' 'Maybe,' you said, 'whenever one of my books comes out.' You didn't notice you were now alone, in front of glasses of lemonade with rosewater, until she said she had lost all those she had loved and that she had only her children left. Apparently you had made a reference to the black dress she was wearing. You thought of that ancient line of poetry: 'Those I love are gone and I am left solitary, like a sword.' But you didn't say it. Your mind, quite separately from you, summoned up the words of the poem, which didn't normally come to mind, and the line tripped across your silent tongue word by word. The line took hold of you and you couldn't drive it out of your head. That saddened you, or upset you, you don't know, and you told her, 'At least you have your children.' When you uttered this stupid comment you broke free of the line of poetry and relaxed. But she ignored the comment and said, 'It's not true what you wrote in your book *Hamiya and the Bridge*.' You asked her what she meant exactly. She spoke about how the woman you had loved in your country asked you for a divorce shortly after you escaped abroad. She was referring to one of the chapters in your previous book, which was a mixture of autobiography and fiction. You told her the book was not a documentary work, not a real autobiography, because it had imaginary elements, perhaps more than it drew from reality. She said something to the effect that even if the book was entirely fictional, that didn't change the fact that the woman you were talking about had not sought a divorce soon or in the way you described.

You remembered your contract of marriage to Roula, which you had found among your papers. It was dated about six months before your sudden flight. The conversation between you finally seemed to be on the right track. You felt comfortable and you felt no urge to cough.

You don't know how long you went on talking. Then the lights came on. Roula pulled down the hem of her dress, which had ridden up above her knees, exposing two round, well-formed, wheaten thighs that you knew well. 'My deepest condolences!' you heard her say, referring to your wife.

X

You had to face the person you had long avoided, the one you left behind twenty years ago. Or, more precisely, the one who hadn't crossed the border with you to the City Overlooking the Sea, and had not lived the life you had lived since that moment. The one you hadn't dragged with you from country to country, along with a small suitcase and a few books, the one who had not known the cold that had chilled you to the bone, who had not seen wars and sieges and how people can eat rats and cats, who had not seen the victims of the plague staggering in the streets and falling on the pavements like autumn leaves. You knew that confrontation was inevitable with this person, who would turn up at the worst of times, fold his arms across his chest, and scrutinise you like an obstinate examiner. He's not a ghost. But also he's not flesh and blood. You find it hard to define his status. He exists and that's it. He's here, exactly as you left him.

That night you sat alone, as usual, on the balcony after the rest of the family had gone to bed one by one. The coughing and the insomnia, which had disappeared on your first nights, now recurred. Your remaining family did not stay up late on the balcony as they did in the old days. The nights of the past now came back to you, with their smells, the carefree laughter, the stories told in three or four versions. Your grandfather's version. Your grandmother's version. Your father's version. Your mother's version. It was usually the last version that decided between the other versions, because your mother had an extraordinary memory and could reconstruct faces, events and words with an accuracy unrivalled by anyone else in the family or in the neighbourhood. You felt there was someone hovering around you. There was someone waiting for this opportunity. Maybe you were waiting too.

You knew that if he spoke he wouldn't stop. If he stopped it would be hard to persuade him to speak again. You also knew that you were the one expected to speak. You first. Because you were required to tell a story that matched his story. A story justifying what had happened. Then you might be quits in his eyes: a story that settles the score after another story. But can one story mend the ruptures, patch up the holes in a life that has almost run its course? Is there a story that is the mother of all stories? An overall story. You don't know. But nonetheless it's definitely you that has to speak first. Go on, tell him one of the stories from your exile, your life abroad, your wanderings (call it what you like), or make one up for him. But what should you talk about? About promises, hopes, wars and sieges, the wandering life, the cold, waning vigour, sadness and death the reaper? That's too much. Besides, you're scatterbrained and disorganised. There is a story that might not make him very happy but it might hold his attention. It's about the man who split in two. Of course he knows that story. But you don't mean you and him, but rather you and the person whose name was the same as your pseudonym, who wrote in newspapers like you and who chased you tirelessly through a labyrinthine city of twisting lanes because he wanted to find out who had assumed his identity. Tell him that story, even if you don't know what his reaction will be, but stipulate that he must listen to you till the end. Stipulate that he cannot interrupt. That way you can keep him under control if he rebels. You can sidestep his questions when you don't have a satisfactory answer. You can take him on a wild goose chase with your convoluted story. You're in a good mood now. Take advantage of it.

You sat up straight on the mattress on the floor. You cleared your throat. Then you told him, 'Listen to me as long as your bad temper will permit. A meeting like this, face to face in the open air, with all the time in the world, doesn't always happen, and may not happen often in the future. You don't know everyone I know but I definitely know everyone you know. You don't know, for example, that I'm not the only person who uses this pseudonym, which you don't like. How could you know that there's someone else who's a professional writer, like me, and bears the same name as me but who lives, fortunately, far away where the ocean roars and a thousand deserts loom? We have never lived in the same place. I myself only noticed this when I was asked to explain how I could be in two places or with two different women at the same time, although I am not some kind of superman. Then I was asked how I had come to write things that weren't like me and that don't bear the hallmark of my nervous tension, which is more famous than my writing itself. This is apart from the fact that his writings on current affairs take a position that is different from mine. I didn't believe the talk about these alleged writings until a friend showed me some cuttings of them and I found that the content and form had nothing to do with me. They weren't better than what I write, or worse. They were just completely different. It's true that language is a universal feature of humanity and the same ideas are widely available, but the way we handle words and ideas differs from one person to another.

'The first time I noticed that this person existed was when a critic, in the country that stretches from the ocean to the desert, commended my book *Hamiya and the Bridge* and I found a blurred photograph published with the review. The photo department in the newspaper had assumed it was a picture of me. It wasn't me. I was convinced of that even though the picture was blurred and didn't have any distinguishing features, unless you count the thick glasses that almost covered the man's eyes. But when I remembered that I do sometimes wear thick-framed glasses, I was a little hesitant about taking a position on the identity of the person in the photograph. I interpreted it as just a coincidence. There was someone else whose name was my pseudonym and who practised the same profession. They say that God can create forty likenesses of a single person, so it wouldn't be hard for Him to inspire forty men (or women) to give their children my assumed name, which you don't like. I don't know if you knew this, but when I gave myself this name, after I fled the country, I was thinking only that it was ordinary, a name like any other name.'

You stopped talking, then you looked at him. His face showed signs of scepticism, as though he wanted to say something. But apparently he intended to comply with your stipulation, not to interrupt until the end. So you continued:

'Please believe me. Yes. That was the reason. After we split in two, I wanted to have an ordinary name that wouldn't draw attention, that wouldn't arouse suspicion of any kind and that was plausible in that city where bullets could easily fly. A name that would be lost among other names, with no special meaning, though in our language it's hard for names not to have meanings or symbolise something. For example, my first name (which is now exclusively yours and which I remember only when I'm with you on this balcony or in the troubling dreams I have) is the name of a prophet, a man who's also known as Jonah. But a marginal prophet. I don't know what his message was. It's said that in Nineveh he tried to guide his people to the right path but didn't succeed. He abandoned them. He wandered around aimlessly. He went to sea and a whale swallowed him. I don't think my father meant to imply any of this when he called me Younis. It would be disastrous if that's what he intended, because there's nothing of Younis the prophet in me, or even of Younis our relative, a good man we never saw without his crutches. Anyway I don't like this name. It always struck me as an old man's name. For ages it reminded me of our relative, who was already old when he was born. On crutches. This is the truth that you in particular must know. Besides, I don't like big names. The names of heroes and gods that some writers and poets and politicians working in revolutions and secret organisations adopt for themselves. You know that in Hamiya I was branded with a red-hot iron on my stomach because of books and ideas, and I didn't choose for myself (sorry, I mean you didn't choose for yourself, because I still mix up the two personalities and the two periods) a name other than Younis al-Khattat. I want you to know you're not the only one to have suffered. The anxiety and uncertainty I went through were no less painful than the disappointment, the sense of abandonment and neglect that you suffered. To carry around someone you no longer are, a name you're not known by among people but which nonetheless remains stuck to you, is not just a procedural matter. Do you understand? It's not just a question of a passport and bureaucracy. If that were the case, it wouldn't be a subject worth talking about now.'

Once again you noticed the anticipation on his face. He didn't ask you in words. But the expression on his face was asking for a clarification. The expression was telling you that the two things didn't balance out. One of them was unlike the other. You looked uncertain too. Because one cannot fully express what one feels. There's no language in the world that can convey feelings as they stir and shift inside us, especially if they arise from uncertainty and confusion. So you continued:

'How can I best explain it to you? I could just tell you it's an existential question. A question of existing or not existing. In other words, of you being yourself and someone else at the same time. And this is something you didn't know. But trust me when I say that it doesn't matter what we call the suffering as long as it comes from the same painful source. Of course there's more than one reason why I'm sharing secrets with you twenty years after we split up, and the most important one is for amusement. Because the nights are long on this balcony, which is open to a star-studded sky. The nights are long here and we don't have anything else to do. Our father died of grief at how I damaged his reputation. That's what you told me with unenviable arrogance. Although I doubt that. Our mother died after him. And before them our grandfather and grandmother. It was they who would ensure the evening passed quickly by telling stories, and besides we're no longer so young that we need compete to count the stars, which we were forbidden to count in the old days in case warts appeared on our hands. Do you remember that? We used to count a particular patch of sky, then discover that we were counting the same stars again, or that the patch had started to grow bigger and the number of stars was multiplying, or they were changing their positions and their shapes. So we would stop counting, happily admitting defeat. So let me tell you my story about the other man who has that name of mine you don't like. It might amuse you. Or console you. And it might persuade you to tell me a story, maybe about the little tricks you play, about how you're still not cured of love, and about your letters to Roula, which more than once have put me in an embarrassing and awkward position. I know you're still writing them, with inspiration from the Song of Solomon, which I can no longer stand, because they find their way to me in the far reaches of exile.'

You noticed that he raised his eyebrows in protest. So you told him, 'Stop that. Do you think I don't know who keeps writing the love letters, even if you don't always send them? Don't raise your eyebrows. Stop shaking your head and let me continue.' He did in fact stop making those gestures of protest, but with a certain pain, which showed in his eyes. You felt sorry for him. To ease the situation, you told him, 'Do you want to know how my meeting with Roula went?' You saw his features relax and his hands, which were clasped tight across his chest, loosen up. You told him, 'I'll tell you, provided I can go back to my story. Will you promise me that?' He nodded in agreement in a childish manner that made you feel even more sorry for him. You told him:

'Firstly, it was you who loved her, not me. It's true that I didn't completely break free of you, if you'll forgive the expression, because something of you survived inside me. But I don't know exactly what it was. When I stood in front of the mirror I felt anxious inside. I took a tranquilliser. Then I relaxed a little. But it wasn't the tranquilliser that made me feel that the whole business was something to do with someone else. With you, to be precise. Because the pill wasn't hallucinogenic. There are such pills that make one hallucinate and see things that in reality don't exist. No, it was an ordinary tranquilliser. And I've grown used to taking them to calm my nerves and make the images that go through my mind less intense. It's a disease or a symptom that's called "depression" and it's common these days, but these pills in any case no longer do me much good. It was you who stood looking at me in the mirror. Don't wave your hand in denial. Don't do it. Because I know it. Why? Firstly, because we really have become different people – the one here that's you, and the one there that's me. Even when I came back I didn't become you, and I don't think we will become one again. Secondly, if it was up to me, I wouldn't have let my eyes climb up her legs and try to move her dress up her golden thighs, so much so that I lost track of what she was saying. If it mattered to me as much as it mattered to you, I would have kept looking at her face, despite the ravages of ruthless time. Thirdly, she referred to the fact that she always sees Younis al-Khattat. She doesn't need a newspaper or magazine to see him and be aware of him, because he never left here as I did. Yes. She said she's kept every line he wrote. Every sprig of lavender he picked from the flowerbeds in the Hamiya gardens. The newspaper in which the poem 'Lady of the City' appeared. She said these things were her treasures. That she called her first son Badr after his favourite poet. And then it doesn't require extraordinary intelligence to realise that I've changed, become

164

a different person in fact, with a different life and different relationships and interests from Younis al-Khattat. This didn't escape her. Because she loved Younis al-Khattat, and Younis al-Khattat isn't me. So let me go back to the first story. You don't seem enthusiastic but listen to me anyway.

'The local newspapers started to write about me, but as someone other than you, after the Grandson died and the censorship of publications was lifted. You know from the papers that I travel often and I'm invited to conferences and meetings. Sometimes I recite poetry that doesn't follow the traditional rules of metre or rhyme, poetry such as you've never written and that maybe you don't consider poetry, or I make fiery comments about change and the transition from the old slow-moving times to new times (I no longer do this because I've been losing faith in many things), or I take part in meetings on narrative and biography. Anyway, some years ago I was invited to a conference in an old city with houses that lean against each other and with markets and alleyways that crisscross like a tangle of intestines. Like a body, it had orifices that were open and hidden at the same time. This is roughly how it was described by a foreign woman who visited it and was cured of insomnia and chronic emotional trauma. In my case, I can say that the houses, the alleyways and cafés of the city, where people had lived and breathed non-stop for a thousand years, brought back memories of cities where I had lived shortly after we split. It was the smell of mint, rose-water and marzipan from the houses and cafés in the afternoons that set my memory working in reverse. So did the smell of manure from the animals that were still the only means of transport in the markets and streets, which were so narrow that they hardly allowed two people to pass. Don't be surprised that such a city still exists on the face of our wretched planet. What I say is not a figment of my imagination, because that doesn't obey me much any longer. The city exists, exactly as I'm describing it to you. I can imagine right now the man who makes leather shoes, whose small shop smelt of tanning, sitting on the doorstep of his house (I don't know how I found my way there through the maze of alleyways and interlocking houses), drinking mint tea from a greenish glass veined with golden lines, smoking cigarette after cigarette and staring perhaps at the same stars we can see arrayed above us here. I can imagine that. When he found out I hailed from a country near the Holy Land, he invited me to his house in the hope I would bring him good luck. Imagine? Me bring him good luck, when I'm weighed down by doubts and sins, a mixture of atheism and an early religious upbringing!'

He looked like he was about to break his promise to listen to you till the end. He seemed to be growing annoyed. He probably wanted you to get on with the story rather than twisting and turning around it, so you continued:

'No story is straightforward. Time isn't straightforward either. Because time and words and emotions wrap around each other like the layout of that ancient city, or like some of your father's calligraphic designs, which turn words into eternal riddles. But, in deference to your impatience, which remains unchanged, I will summarise:

'Our hosts put us up in a hotel that was once the home of a city notable but had been sold by his grandchildren to some of the investors who flocked to the city when it became an international tourist destination. Now you can hear people jabbering in multiple languages in the city's lanes and markets, where one might easily get lost for ever. The hotel, I mean the home of the notable, was built in the style of the great king-doms that came and went in that region. It had a high wooden gate carved with images of imaginary birds and delicate flow-ers that one could almost smell. A mounted horseman could have ridden through the gate without bending down. In the middle of the courtyard there was a pool, with a fountain in the centre. The tiles on the floor of the courtyard and in the pool were very small. The patterns they formed changed every ten or fifteen tiles, depending on the angle of inclination of the sun, and even in the dark they reflected colours that varied between green and blue and pale yellow, as though the pool and the tiles that were in it and around it reflected a traveller's dream about a place he sought but could not reach. In the courtyard I found people I knew and others I didn't. I was given an upper room that overlooked the pool. In fact all the rooms overlooked the pool. I put my bag in the room. Leaning over the marble basin, I washed my face slowly with the water of the city. Because, despite everything, I still see water as a source of good luck, just as my grandmother did. I see water as able to bring the dead back to life and, when I wash, I repeat some of her ritual prayers silently to myself. Then I went down to the courtyard. The guests were milling around, chatting away at various levels and pitches, without them noticing the changing patterns of the tiles or the shifts in their colours as the sun moved across the sky. I drank a frothy mint tea, served by a boy in traditional costume, carrying a teapot that never ran dry on a pale silver tray that never ran out of glasses. I stood with a friend who comes from a country close to our country. Behind my back I heard someone say, "Have you seen Adham Jaber?" I looked back. The other person pointed at me, and the person who had asked said, "No, that's not him." Then they melted into the crowd. My friend noticed that something had come over me. "Is there a problem?" he asked. "No," I said. Then, after a short silence, I added, "Did you hear someone mention my name?" "No, I didn't," he said. I thought that what I had heard was a hallucination, like the ones I have that are a mixture of fantasy and reality. But in the lobby, in the lecture hall, on our magical tour through the warren of twisting lanes in the old city, and in the restaurant, I still felt that there were eyes pinned on me at all times. I heard my name mentioned several times, but they were not referring to me. I didn't think much about it. I left it as it was in its raw state. In all its mystery, real or imaginary. Sometimes I do that. I just let the feeling sink in without allowing my mind to analyse it. But the eyes pursuing me had come closer and grown more piercing. I could almost feel them penetrating every inch of me. The breath I could feel behind my back, which disappeared when I turned around, was almost stinging. Breaths interspersed by a feeble wheezing sound, from lungs ruined by nicotine. I hadn't done anything here to deserve being monitored by anyone. Nothing real called for that, especially in this place. Because I'm far from Hamiya, very far, and what I did there is of no interest to anyone here. On the eve of the conclusion of the conference, I had a headache. You don't know those headaches that knock me out. I wanted to have a rest in my room before joining the group for the traditional closing ceremony that the organisers had prepared. I went to reception to get the key to my room. The receptionist was speaking to a man who, from the back, seemed to be on the stout side. I heard the receptionist tell the man with some impatience, "Sir, there's no one on the guest list by that name, and the only person from that city is Mr

Younis." Then the receptionist saw me approaching. The other man turned to see where the receptionist was looking, and the receptionist said, "There he is!" Before I could reach the wooden counter behind which he was standing, the receptionist asked me, as if pleading for help, "Mr Younis, has anyone other than you come from the city where you live?" I looked straight at the man, who resembled to some extent the man whose picture was published with the article praising my book. "No," I said, "I'm the only one."

'The man was taken aback by my sudden arrival. I assumed he felt embarrassed by what the receptionist had done. He was wearing glasses that seemed thicker than in the blurry photograph. I was about his height when I stood next to him. He smiled at me. His smile conveyed a message I guessed at immediately. A message I had been expecting ever since I realised there were eyes following me in the hallway, in the lobby, in the lecture room, on our magical tour through the winding lanes of the old city, in the restaurant. The man with the glasses put out a fat, hairy hand and said, "Pleased to meet you, Mr Younis." Then, emphasising all the consonants, he added, "I'm Adham Jaber!"'

XI

In his first days back home he did no more than laze around and browse through his papers, old books and photo albums. Maybe it was a deliberate attempt to reconnect with the past, or perhaps to distract his mind from what had happened in the City of Red and Grey. His family didn't ask him about what had happened, whether he was ill or not, or about the coughing fits he had, or the pocket handkerchiefs he was always changing, or why his face was so pale. They left him time to tell them about all that, but I know he didn't forget the images of people staggering down the streets, the coughing, the blood they spat out, the faces covered in masks and the X signs marked on particular houses. Sometimes these images were combined with images of death and destruction in the City of Siege and War, of people hugging the walls for cover against the constant shelling, or looking for something to eat in the rubbish bins.

He knew how he was, and he didn't want to waste time.
He drew up a plan in his head and decided to carry it out.

He rediscovered the summer house, which had become the family's base after his father retired. He knew that their neighbours in the housing estate, which the Grandson had given to an elite of junior officers and civil servants, and which had now become a large town, were originally his relatives and acquaintances of his family. That was no longer the case. The Hamiya civil servants had mixed with people who worked in the 'free city' that had been built near by. This surprised him somewhat. Accompanied by young Younis, he continued to go round the bedrooms and reception rooms in the house. He would sit for a time in his own room, which his family had preserved roughly as it was, then go to the kitchen in the hope of reconnecting with old habits he had known, smells that still nestled in his nose and in his memory, or of rediscovering his father in the cellar.

He clearly tried to make up for his neglect of his father's works by taking a fresh look at them. He spent a long time in his father's workshop. Sometimes young Younis would swoop down the twelve stairs with him like a little bundle of energy, but sometimes he would give his nephew the slip and sneak into his father's temple alone. Young Younis was so firmly attached to his legendary uncle who had come to life after long wanderings that he brought him the grandfather's white cotton skullcap and put it on his head, just as grandfather used to wear it. The skill and precision of his father's handiwork amazed him. He saw lines he had never seen before. Innovations in the *thuluth* style, experiments with the *mansoub*, in which there is a fixed geometrical proportion between the letters and the letter *alif*, softened versions of the harsh Kufic style with its perpendicular letters and square blocks. There were a few works by his grandfather too. Less severe and less observant of the rules. Like lessons in calligraphy. Long sentences. Black and white were dominant. Ornamental elements. They seemed to be independent of the text itself. Lots of decoration and foliage. Almost no empty spaces. The *thuluth* that fascinated his father had also fascinated his grandfather. He stood in front of his grandfather's design. He smiled, then laughed. It bore a common line of poetry: *Do not regret the treachery of time, for many a dog has danced on the corpses of lions!* He liked dogs. He remembered his dog Antar, who had died shortly before he came back, as if he had been waiting for him. But dogs don't live long. Antar lived close to twenty years and that's a long life for a dog in our country. He had seen lions only in zoos or in pictures but he had definitely seen many dogs wherever he lived. He thought about the metaphor 'the treachery of time' in his grandfather's design. It wasn't the word 'treachery' that caught his attention but the circularity of time. Actions and consequences. The cycle of the body and the cycle of the seasons. He knew how his father admired Ibn Muqla, whose name he heard often in the Thursday salons. He used to call him 'the master of calligraphy'. He tried to remember who wrote that frightening sentence that went, *No blood money for a hand that does not write*. He didn't know. He used to hear his father quote the saying, sometimes with a kind of irony. Whenever he heard his father say it, he thought it was aimed at him. But his father didn't mean him. In fact his father didn't agree with the saying. In the cellar he found many of his late father's notebooks. Some of them contained what looked like notes or diaries. In others there were comments on previous works and on his contemporaries, and quotations from various people, some named and some not. Perhaps the latter were his father's. He browsed through the notebooks, then put them aside. He was frightened of finding something that would spoil the pleasure of the moment, particularly something about their own charged relationship. He put them aside as if to say, 'Not now.' He started to read his father's notebooks on calligraphy and calligraphers. In one of the notebooks he read what looked like a summary of Ibn Muqla's calligraphic masterpieces and vignettes of his life, which fluctuated dramatically between high points and low points. Apparently Ibn Muqla's strident fame eclipsed any mention of his brother, Abu Abdullah, who also excelled in calligraphy. His father suggested in passing that the two brothers devised some twenty-four scripts, of which he mentioned six: the *thuluth*, the *rihan*, the *tawqia*, the *muhaqqaq*, the *badia* and the *riqaa*. But his father only mentioned Ibn Muqla when he wrote about his theory of the geometry of calligraphy. His father wrote, 'The Master of Calligraphy was inspired by a heavenly idea that started with the dot and the circle. He took the height of the letter *alif* as the diameter of the circle and correlated all the other letters to it.' His father speculated, '*Alif* is the first letter in the Arabic alphabet and also the first letter in the name of God, Allah. The *alif* and the circle are both tokens of the absolute.' His father, or maybe someone else, wrote this phrase: 'It is the trunk, and everything else is a branch.'

He was surprised at the fate in store for Ibn Muqla. He hadn't known he had gone through such ordeals and faced death so many times in such strange ways. He was vizier to three caliphs: al-Muqtadir Billah, al-Qahir Billah and al-Radi Billah. He was exiled three times, died three deaths and was buried in three graves. First he was buried in a well, then his corpse was dug up and buried in his son's house, then it was dug up again and buried in his wife's house. During his life he underwent oppression, political persecution and the confiscation of his assets, and his end was appalling. He was denounced to al-Radi Billah and his right hand was cut off. In his dark cell, the calligraphic master of his age said, 'A hand with which I served caliphs and copied the Holy Quran, cut off like the hand of a thief?!'

He didn't know what the denunciation was that cost Ibn Muqla his hand. His father didn't mention it in the notebook in which he summarised part of Ibn Muqla's life and the foundations of calligraphy that he had set out. There were sayings. Lines of poetry. Including this line that his father attributed to the Master of Calligraphy when his hand was cut off: 'If part of you dies, weep for it, because the part that has died is close to the part that is left.' The strange thing is that, after his hand was cut off, his tongue was also cut out and he was jailed and remained in prison until he 'surrendered his soul to his Creator' – that was precisely his father's expression. He wondered, 'Why did they cut out his tongue? His hand was his weapon. Cutting it off made sense. But why did they cut out his tongue? Was it because he was outspoken? Or to deprive him of any form of human expression?' He didn't know. Many people apparently wrote elegies for him too. Including al-Sahib ibn Ibad, who said, 'The calligraphy of the vizier Ibn Muqla was a delight to the heart and to the eye.' But his father, writing what amounted to a short biography of this extraordinary calligrapher, concentrated on his calligraphic works and largely ignored the man's ruthless pursuit of luxury, prestige and power. The man seemed quite the antithesis of his father. More like our intellectuals today, in their relationships with authority and rulers. It occurred to him that events recur in a vicious cycle. The subject preoccupied him. It reinvigorated him. He didn't need to go to the public library to find out more about Ibn Muqla. In his father's library there were several reference books, both classical and modern, on the pioneers of Arabic calligraphy and aspects of their lives. There he saw the calligrapher's other face. He found out why he was imprisoned, and why his hand was cut off and then his tongue. It was a troubled period with many intrigues and conspiracies, and the Abbasid empire was starting to fall apart. It seems that the historian Ibn Kathir hated Ibn Muqla. Hated his character, probably not his calligraphy. He said Ibn Muqla was hapless and impecunious in early life. But he managed to accumulate wealth, which he then began to spend lavishly. He began his political life collecting the land tax from parts of Persia, and his business affairs turned from bad to good, and from good to better, and his good reputation reached the ears of the caliph al-Muqtadir. When the office of vizier fell vacant after Ali ibn Issa, three candidates were proposed to the caliph: al-Fadl ibn Jaafar ibn al-Furat, Abu Ali ibn Muqla and Muhammad ibn Khalaf al-Nirmani. The three names did not appeal to the caliph's entourage, because for each one of them there was some story or some good reason why he was unacceptable. They told al-Muqtadir, 'As for Ibn al-Furat, we killed his uncle, the vizier Abul Hassan, and his nephew, and we confiscated his sister's property, so we don't feel safe with him. As for Ibn Muqla, he's a complete novice with no experience in the vizierate and no prestige among the people. As for Muhammad ibn Khalaf al-Nirmani, he's an irresponsible ignoramus who's no good at secretarial work or scholarship.' But the fact that al-Muqtadir's entourage rejected Ibn Muqla's name did not discourage the power-hungry master of calligraphy. He was shrewd. He was determined to catch the caliph's attention by any means possible. He wanted to become vizier whatever happened. But how? He went to the town of Anbar with fifty homing pigeons to carry reports of the constant intrigues and conspiracies that came close to threatening the caliphate itself. News of the far-flung empire came to him on the wings of the fifty birds that had been dispersed in all four directions, and he would pass the news on to al-Muqtadir's office. Finally, some of the caliph's aides said to the caliph, 'Ibn Muqla has done this on his own initiative, so how would he perform if you actually gave him a job?' So the caliph gave him the vizierate on the basis of what he had heard about him. Reading all this in the basement, he was struck by Ibn Muqla's infatuation with birds. Why birds in particular? He didn't know, but he read an amusing story about how the calligrapher, when he was vizier, became obsessed with breeding animals in general, and birds in particular. One of the reference books said he had a large and flourishing garden that he filled with rare trees, birds and other animals. The net he used to cover the garden was made of silk. Under the net there were types of birds beyond description. Ibn al-Jawfi wrote about this garden and its unique contents, and noted that in it he bred birds which are usually bred only on farms, such as various types of turtle dove and wild pigeon, as well as nightingales, parrots, bulbuls, peacocks and partridge. There were also gazelles, wild cows, ostriches, camels and wild donkeys, which made it a zoo that was comprehensive for its time. One day one of his workers saw a seabird mating with a land bird. He monitored them and when the female laid eggs and the eggs started to hatch, he rushed to Ibn Muqla and told him what had happened. Ibn Muqla gave the worker a hundred dinars as a bonus for bringing him the news. After he had read extracts from the biography of the man who founded the discipline of Arabic calligraphy, the question that overwhelmed him was this: How did Ibn Muqla find time to invent twenty-four scripts? How did he manage to bring about the great leap from one stage to another in the progress of calligraphy when he spent most of his time manoeuvring, arguing, forming alliances and hatching conspiracies in order to obtain the office of vizier?

He knew of his father's interest in al-Suhrawardi, but he didn't know he had spent so much time collecting and editing his works. Al-Suhrawardi's works have never been published in a single collection. In Arabic he is known mainly for his famous poem with *ha'* as the rhyme letter. He knew most of the lines by heart, but not for the same reason as his father. He discovered that his father had made good progress collecting al-Suhrawardi's poems and poetic fragments from three manuscripts, one of which was preserved in the al-Zahiriya Library and numbered 5576. The second was in the Berlin Museum numbered 7669, and the third includes an extension of the ancient poem that begins *Suad appeared* and is in Tubingen with the number R137. He also found a letter from the director of the Berlin Museum, signed Dr George. The first manuscript is written in a Persian-style script, the second and third in *naskh*. There is also an unfinished copy in *thuluth* that his father had started to write out, based on the poems available to him by the Sufi master, who is said to have been killed by Saladin or his son. His father opened the manuscript with a quotation that goes: *He who seeks the truth by means of proof is like someone who finds the way to the sun by means of a lantern.* There's no attribution for this saying but it must be Suhrawardi's. The truth. Proof. The inner and the outer truth again.

He stood for a long time in front of a calligraphic design written in the *thuluth jali* script and his heart pounded. It was a poem that read:

Life has no savour now that you have taken leave of it,
The night has no magic now that you are gone.

He thought the poem was about him.

Did his father write this poem in excellent *thuluth jali* about him?

Was his father's life after the flight of his rebellious son without savour, and his nights, after he was gone, without magic?

His feeling didn't change when he discovered that the line was by al-Sharif al-Radi in mourning for Ibn al-Bawwab, the master of calligraphy who came after Ibn Muqla. He told himself his father was in the habit of writing things in which he read a second meaning. It also surprised him that young Younis could read the riddles in the Kufic design that hung in the corner by the entrance to the cellar. He had learned from young Younis things he hadn't given himself a chance to learn when he was twenty years old. The fact that the child had outdone him didn't necessarily mean he was more intelligent. He may have learned the secret of the Kufic labyrinth from his father Shihab, who was very close to his father, or because the boy himself was attached to his grandfather, who had passed away when he was four or five years old. 'It's either familiarity or repetition,' he told himself.

He had to visit the house where he found his feet as a child, the house where he left his family when he took flight into the unknown. On the great journey from which people, if they return at all, do not return as they were. Everyone expected him to visit the house. He didn't take anyone with him on the tour of inspection of his old haunts. He went alone. He came back dripping with sweat and stifling constant bouts of coughing with his handkerchief. He closed the door of his room and did not come out for the rest of the day. He didn't tell his brother Shihab about the trip, but everyone knew he had gone. In one of our lengthy exchanges on the balcony of our house, he told me in surprise how he found the old banned books, the ones that many people were once punished for possessing, on display at the pavement bookstalls in the commercial centre, covered in dust, next to books on cooking and interior design. He told me he couldn't understand how the books were on display like that, in broad daylight, while other books that used to be on display on the pavements, and that no one read, were now deemed more dangerous than drugs. He said time had a strange cycle, and ideas had even stranger cycles. He recalled the proverb that says that every age has its dynasty and its heroes, to which he added his own observation: 'and its ideas too'. Because how was it that a book such as *The State and Revolution*, which had left an indelible scar on his stomach, could be displayed in the middle of the pavement, next to the feet of passers-by, while books such as *Governance is God's*, *The Hejab is a Sharia Requirement*, *Sacred Jihad* and other books that used to be on sale openly were now more dangerous than heroin? He wasn't unaware of the changes that had taken place here, but he was surprised by the dramatic transformation of the Grandson's allies into dangerous enemies. Enemies who had once held an honoured place in the alliance against poisonous imported ideas but who had now descended into dark cellars where they turn the bodies of their young men into bombs. Because in the days when people like him were being hunted down and thrown in jail, the former allies of the Grandson had been preoccupied with fatwas about sexual intercourse and with debating what would invalidate their Ramadan fast or their ritual ablutions before prayer. 'Praise be to the One Who brings about change,' he said, as if someone other than himself was uttering the words.

Two or three days after he arrived, a luxury car stopped in front of the house. A young man wearing a suit and a large tie got out. The man asked for him, and he came out to meet him. The young man was one of Mahmoud Abu Tawila's staff. He wanted to take him to meet his old comrade. He declined, saying he wasn't able to go. He asked him to tell his boss he would see him as soon as he was done with his various engagements. Clearly he didn't want to meet his old comrade, at least not in the first few days after returning. The next day the same car stopped in front of the house again. A tall man got out, well-dressed with a trimmed black moustache and short jet-black hair. It was Mahmoud Abu Tawila. It was no longer possible to avoid meeting him. He didn't go off with him, but invited him into the same diwan where his old comrade had previously attended some of the evening salons. Mahmoud Abu Tawila seemed humbled when he saw the picture of the father. He stood a while in front of the calligraphies hanging on the walls. He said things about how the country had lost a rare talent. 'May God have mercy on his soul,' he added. In a tone that may or may not have been sincere, he said, 'The time has come for our country to embrace creativity, not drive it away!' As with many things, he couldn't be sure of his former comrade's feelings towards his father. There was that constant ambiguity in the tone of his voice and in the way he spoke, the effortless way he patched together common sayings, maxims, proverbs and his own linguistic innovations to create what sounded like a model page from a textbook, though not one that was circulated widely. I gathered that Mahmoud offered him work in the cultural or media departments, as with other former opposition people. He added a new refrain to what he had said about change from within when they had met by chance in the City of Red and Grey. He told him the whole country was now at a crossroads, that the map of the region was being redrawn and they had to preserve the country's identity and unity. He said the new commander did not have the experience or even the charisma of the Grandson, so it was essential to strengthen the national institutions that guaranteed the unity of the country and its survival in the face of the coming storm. He understood that his friend Mahmoud really was worried that a fragmentation of Hamiya's nucleus, under pressure from the changes in the region, would lead to the wholesale disintegration of the country. Mahmoud told him that the country was at the centre of a tug-of-war between two camps, which political circles called the old guard and the new guard. Although he rejected the terminology, he was inclined towards those described as the old guard and said the label did not offend him. They were the ones, he said, who could be relied on to defend the identity and unity of the country. He told him that labels don't usually mean much but in this case they did. The label was pejorative, as he put it, intended to give the impression, especially abroad, that this camp was reactionary and that its leading members were lured by the medals and other decorations that covered the

Grandson's chest, but in fact those known as the 'new guard' were just a bunch of political buffoons suddenly parachuted into the country by murky financiers. They weren't very different from a group whose name might ring a bell with him, *compradors*, and that was what they were now being called by local radicals of the kind that exist in every age, even at this moment of major turbulence that was sweeping away ideas and ideologies. He didn't comment on what his old friend said. It struck him as remote from his immediate concerns, as if Mahmoud were talking about things that were happening on another planet. Inside, he was surprised at how emotionally detached he was from what was happening in his country, if it really was happening, that is. He realised that history had its decisive moments and that this was doubtless one of them. So how was it that everyone remained indifferent to the bleak picture his old friend painted of the country's future? He didn't want to say anything. This probably stemmed from his inability to respond, not from an aversion to speaking or because he rejected what he was hearing from his old friend, who had preserved his extraordinary inner energy. He was familiar with those nihilistic moments when he felt indifferent towards things, when moving was the same as staying still, when speaking was the same as silence, right the same as wrong. That internal paralysis that a psychiatrist he often went to in the City of Red and Grey had linked to chronic depression.

Is that what he had?

He politely ignored Mahmoud's offer. But Mahmoud didn't give up. He wasn't that type. He asked him to think it over and said he understood his circumstances after everything he'd been through. He told him the country needed him now more than ever. He, personally, needed his advice. But he avoided a candid response to Mahmoud's request and said he wanted to be free at last to write. He had many post-poned projects and needed time to finish them off. His old friend noticed that he wasn't in good shape. He didn't look like the person he had met again in the City of Red and Grey ten years after they had parted. Mahmoud knew what had happened in that city. He knew what had happened to his wife. As he hinted to his friend who had returned, he also knew that he had been the 'guest' of the National Security Agency. He told him they had nothing against him now because circumstances had changed, the old files had been closed, and the agency now had other priorities. But the returnee was somewhere else, in body and in spirit. He had a plan of action from which he would not deviate. In our lengthy exchanges, he admitted to me that he still harboured some affection for his old friend, who had long competed with him in everything. Because there are some things that can't be wiped out easily, feelings that don't completely dissi-pate or turn into their opposites. There's a sediment that settles in the heart. There's something that lingers in the depths, resisting complete obliteration.

I don't know why one distant memory came back to him, of when he met Hala. He didn't need to tell me about that particular memory. It happened when he was me. It was more about me than about him. I immediately recalled that after-noon under the vine trellis. The interminable heat. The big shade. Awaiting the arrival of the woman who wanted to join the Organisation. The smell of mint that blew in from I don't know where, because at comrade Hanan's bungalow, in front of which we were sitting on plastic chairs, there was nothing but a vine trellis that cast some welcome shade, and some patchy grass growing on wasteland thanks to a leaky water pipe that had never been fixed. Two of the five or six people present – comrade Hanan and me – knew Hala from before. She lived in a house near comrade Hanan's house and Hanan didn't introduce her to us until she was sure she was eligible to join the Organisation. The meeting was social and informal. That's how it should seem to Hala and to the guards that were posted everywhere. Hala arrived carrying a cake. Beads of sweat were forming on her brow and the tip of her nose, which made her look more attractive. Maybe she was flustered because she didn't know most of those present. I had met Hala casually a few times with comrade Hanan and, because of her easy-going nature, our relationship had become uninhibited, with none of the awkwardness or complexes that usually constrain relationships between young men and women in our country. I noticed that she showed an interest in Mahmoud, but he was so malicious that he ignored her interest. In fact he ignored her completely. I knew this characteristic of his. The way that, by ignoring someone, he makes the person he ignores inquisitive about him. But Hala wasn't the type to be ignored. Her femininity, her cheerfulness, her distinctive Anatolian features, her statuesque figure. It was hard for a young man to see her and not turn his head. But these qualities did not turn Mahmoud's head. That's what he wanted to convey to her, in his devious way. And he succeeded. It was a casual meeting. Various subjects were discussed. But not politics directly, just peripherally: the poverty in the slums and remote towns, women's liberation, eradicating illiteracy, the gaps in the five-year plan and so on. Quick headlines and a cursory discussion. One subject led to another.

That meeting, when Mahmoud spouted what sounded like schoolboy talk on almost every subject that came up, was the start of Hala's infatuation with my friend. The rest is details. Such as the fact that shortly afterwards Hala and Mahmoud announced their engagement, which never came to marriage for some reason he would never disclose to us. I noticed that after the engagement Hala kept her distance and was reserved. She no longer slapped her hand on my shoulder when she laughed at something I had said or kissed me on the cheek when we met. I didn't understand. I asked her if something about me had upset her and she denied it. She said it was maybe because she was tired from work. After graduating from the National Education Institute, the Hamiya personnel department had given her a job as a teacher in a girls' school in a remote town. Her excuse was not convincing. Her attitude upset me but I didn't dwell on it. At the time I was deeply in love with Roula. Her father had been killed and we got engaged after a passionate love affair. Hala's eyes, by clouding over when we met, were telling me why she was keeping her distance, but I ignored them. I found out from comrade Hanan, who told me in disbelief that the reason for Hala's changed behaviour towards me was Mahmoud's jealousy and his suspicion that she was fond of me, or perhaps his suspicion that we had once had a relationship. The mere fact that I had known her before him apparently upset him.

Unfortunately for him, it was only through me that Mahmoud experienced some of the landmark events in his life and developed interests that preoccupied him for so long. This was a pattern that Mahmoud openly fought against. He tried to bury his anger about it deep inside himself, but from time to time it would float to the surface and I could sense the unpleasant taste of it in my stomach. It was apparently too much for him that I had known the woman he was about to marry, even if our acquaintance had gone no further than innocent friendship or affection of the kind that brothers and sisters might have. I must admit he would sometimes startle me with remarks that might not have been original but sounded as if they were. I'll never forget one striking turn of phrase of his, when I told him that he borrowed other people's remarks and brazenly passed them off as his own. 'You shouldn't borrow what you want. You should steal it,' he said.

I didn't bring up the subject of Hala with Mahmoud. Because events gathered pace. How could I have known we were heading towards an event that would drive us apart, that the last memories still resonating in my head would be of this circle of young people full of hope, the leisurely sessions under the vine trellis, and the short man sitting with us who we thought was a senior member of the Organisation while he was in fact the local leader who would later be executed and buried in an unmarked grave? Because what happened happened, and I am no longer me.

He had to make this visit.

It wasn't tradition that made him do it, but something else.

I saw him hurriedly putting on a pair of trousers he took from his wardrobe, then a T-shirt he found on the edge of the bed. He put the hunting hat with the wide brim on his head, the same one he was wearing in the photograph with Khalaf and Salem, after finding it at the top of the wardrobe. He knew the sun would be fierce after a while. He had decided to go and visit them. But his mother and his father were buried in different cemeteries. With the increasing population and the prevalence of death the old cemetery, with its earth graves close to the surface, was crammed full, so a second cemetery and then a third had sprung up. He didn't think about which grave he would visit first but just set off, walking with a slouch. His grey hair flashed like a mirror under the sun of a yawning mid-morning. By his side walked young Younis, sometimes holding his hand, sometimes letting it go, as though uncomfortable with the idea of being connected to someone or something.

Many years ago, when he was the same age and height as the boy who was sometimes holding his hand, sometimes letting it go, he used to walk along these streets, jumping from wall to wall with a stick in his hand. He used to read books about chivalry and the agonies of love under lamp-posts, and comb his hair with a quiff. There were fewer streets then than there are now, but they were tidier. As was apparent from his uncertain gait, he didn't know which street to take after the big junction that divided our district into four equal sections, the junction for which the house that people called Nakuja Abad, after the two words inscribed on the arch outside, was a major landmark. He was looking at the child, and the child realised he was confused. The child pointed towards the west. They crossed the last street he knew and then he left young Younis in charge. He was silent, and so was the boy. From one street to the next, young Younis said, 'This way, Uncle.' Then he would fall silent again. He followed in the footsteps of the boy, who led him by the shortest route, like the word *sakiina* in the maze of his father's Kufic design. I'm sure he gave up trying to recognise the small streets, because the goods in the shops along the way had mostly changed. The new goods met needs that were unknown in the past. Perhaps he noticed that these same goods, with the same names, in the same packets or tins of the same colour, were now available everywhere: an alternative form of internationalism that splashed its brands across towns and villages, across oceans and continents, transcending languages and local distinctions, an internationalism of magic merchandise that floats across the face of the earth.

When he decided to make this visit, he didn't say to me, 'Hey Younis, let's go,' as he did when he visited his friend Salem, who had had a tumour removed from his brain several years ago and lost a considerable part of his memory. His old friend had recognised him briefly, then a moment later asked him who he was. He had also suggested we visit another friend called Wahid, who owns a workshop making metal parts. He's the person who appears in the photograph of the hunting expedition with Khalaf and Salem, the one he didn't recognise at first. He spent longer than I expected with this friend of his. As soon as the man saw him, he said, 'I didn't know that when we daubed horseshit on the governor's car it would become an epic chapter in your book *Hamiya and the Bridge*!' Then, after that quickfire opening, his friend the metal man laughed, revealing teeth decayed by sweet tea and tobacco. The man who had come back to his birthplace also laughed heartily. This was the first carefree laugh I had heard from him since he came back. He laughed until he broke into a protracted coughing fit from deep in his lungs and almost fainted. He likes Wahid. He likes him as much as he liked Khalaf, because they both had reserves of goodwill and loyalty that were impervious to change and unlikely to run out, as if these traits were inseparable parts of their temperament. Something organic that they were born with and would die with. Like hands, heads, noses, hearts and arteries. These two childhood friends of his had not opened a book since they left middle school. Is it books that corrupt, that change and alter deep-rooted nature?

This time he didn't say to me, 'Hey, Younis, let's go.' He took young Younis with him. He asked the boy, 'Do you know where they are?' Without needing to ask his uncle what he meant, the boy said, 'I know. I visit them every Friday and recite the first chapter of the Quran at their graves.'

The cemetery they finally reached hadn't existed before. He didn't recognise it. He knew the old one, which was now in the middle of their neighbourhood. Perhaps he thought that in his time there were fewer dead. Death really had been less familiar, less ordinary than it is today. It was a rare event that brought the whole neighbourhood together. The night after a death was frightening for children, and especially for him. What troubled him most was abandoning the dead after the burial. That communal severance from someone who was alive a few hours earlier. Complete severance. Disengagement. Leaving the body in a hole covered with soil. The worst part is what awaits the dead after that communal severance. An interrogation in which the two angels leave no stone unturned. Various forms of torture if the dead has been undutiful to his parents or has neglected his prayers or fasting. I think he thought of that, because I thought of it, and as long as I thought of it, he must have thought of it too. I began to feel exactly what he felt as soon as he surveyed the large dusty cemetery with its wire fence. The caretaker came out of a wooden hut at the entrance when he saw them pushing the metal gate with the annoying squeak. Young Younis pointed inside the cemetery. When the caretaker shook his head and waved his hands he realised the man couldn't speak. It was clear that the caretaker knew the boy. The sign language that the child used and the caretaker's response certainly looked primitive to the returnee. In the City of Red and Grey, where the person who was me twenty years ago had lived, there had clearly been great progress in sign language. And, of course, even among the deaf there are educated people and illiterates. The caretaker of our cemetery, with his tattered scarf thrown any old how round his neck, might count as a sign-language illiterate. But why would the deaf caretaker of a cemetery, in a place at the mercy of relentless dust, need words beyond those he exchanged with the child? Those few primitive gestures were enough for him to know what the child said, or more precisely what he meant.

The man who had come home couldn't understand the system on which the cemetery was based. The graves, some of them made of earth raised a little above ground level and others on which the family of the dead had had concrete platforms built, took up all the space available. They were cheek by jowl, like the houses in the neighbourhood. But the burials were apparently in chronological order, from the oldest to the most recent. He thought about how the cemetery had become a copy of the very neighbourhoods where he ran through the lanes in his childhood and that remained almost as they were in the past, with the difference that curved aluminium dishes had sprouted on the roofs of houses, like desert mushrooms after abundant rainfall.

At last the boy reached the grave, three steps ahead of his uncle. As soon as his little feet touched the ground in the cemetery, he tried not to step on any of the tightly packed graves, as if picking his way between the arms and legs of a sleeping body he was frightened of awakening from its sacred slumber. The grave was like all the graves around it. Apart from the stone marker, the only thing that distinguished it was an olive tree that received regular doses of water. It was luxuriant. Green, despite the dust that inevitably coated its leaves and branches. In comparison with the olive tree, the other cemetery plants seemed to be yellowing or wilting under a determined sun.

The boy, three paces ahead, looked back with round eyes that said, 'We've arrived!' Then he raised his open hands to the sides of his face and started to mumble. The man who had come home told himself that the boy had been taught the same lessons he had been taught when he was young.

Time can repeat itself.

People can repeat themselves, one way or another.

He noticed that some wild plants with small bright red flowers had sprouted on the grave. Their thin roots had spread inside it. He also noticed that the words inscribed on the tombstone in familiar *thuluth* script were slightly faded, but he could easily read these words: *Here Lies the Late Fatima . . . May She Rest in Peace*. His mother's voice rang in his ears. He remembered that phrase she would use whenever she saw him put a blanket around his shoulders to join his friends for a night out she didn't approve of: 'You'll have a blanket around your shoulders, like a nomad, for the rest of your life.' He remembered what his mother said about devils dancing around him. About his bottom, which wouldn't stay still when he was sitting down, as if he were sitting on a spike or hot coals. Sometimes his mother would sing songs addressed to the birds. He remembered part of a song in which she asked the birds to bring her news of absent loved ones. He didn't know which absent loved ones. Because he hadn't left the nest yet, and Sanad hadn't gone off to the Land of Palm Trees and Oil. He thought that confiding in birds was just a singing tradition his mother had heard from others. Like the introductory lament over abandoned encampments in ancient Arabic poetry. Because in our world birds are associated with travel, perhaps with letters too, and people in our country love to be maudlin for no obvious reason. He remembered other birds, his father's birds, or rather the birds in his books or in his imagination. He had heard the story about them from his father, before reading it later. The birds in which his mother confided had nothing in common with his father's birds. But one thing, as usual, reminds you of something else. That's how wily the memory is, and also one of its disadvantages. At one of those miserable Thursday sessions he heard his father tell his friends the story of the thirty birds and their journey to find themselves a king on Mount Qaf. It was the hoopoe who told the birds where they might find the bird king called the Simorgh: 'He's close to us, and we are far from him. His throne is at the top of a tree that's too tall to see, and no tongue ceases to repeat his name. He is surrounded by a thousand veils, some of light and others of darkness, and no one in creation can grasp his essence!' But the rigours of the journey, which the hoopoe had understated, frightened off the bird that sang, the bird that boasted of its feathers and the bird that relied on its strength, and they all backed out. The birds that agreed to undertake the impossible journey were the least known and the most insignificant in the bird kingdom. Only thirty birds arrive, exhausted and featherless, at Mount Qaf. But the Simorgh, the venerable king of the birds, turns out to be none other than the birds themselves. When the thirty birds look at the Simorgh, he turns out to be the group of thirty birds, and when the birds look at themselves they see the Simorgh.

The sun hung perpendicularly above the grave. An imperious sun that reminded him of the sun he had known here in the old days. He heard the flapping of wings. He looked towards the eastern edge of the cemetery and saw a bird of prey ready to swoop. Beyond the rickety wire fence a spiral of dust was rising into the bare sky and threatening to approach. He noticed that when he heard the flapping of the predator's wings the boy looked in the same direction and saw the spiral of dust. 'We should be going, Uncle,' young Younis said. His uncle didn't answer. He looked at the tombstone and reread the words, carved in black in *thuluth* style: *Here Lies the Late . . .* He looked around the grave. There was no space. No room for another grave. There were graves side by side, without markers. No trees, just some withered weeds. Young Younis stepped towards the cemetery gate where the caretaker, his tattered scarf thrown around his neck, stood looking at them. I had a strong sense that the man who had come home was thinking about himself, about his name, or rather his two names. Which of them would be carved on his tombstone? He looked around, as if looking for someone he could not see but whose presence he sensed. His gaze settled on the east. He coughed violently and spat out blood, lots of blood.

The caretaker was still standing at the ready, his head protected by his scarf from a sun that was starting to grow fiercer. Young Younis had reached the gate. He saw him stop at the entrance. The caretaker went up to the boy and started to talk to him with his hands. As he came up to them young Younis said, 'Uncle, give him something.' The man who had come home automatically put his hand in his trouser pocket

and found a large silver coin, which he handed to the caretaker. The caretaker examined the large silver coin. He turned
it over in his hand and then gave it back, a look of disgust on
his face. He withdrew his right hand sharply. The man who
had come back looked at the coin the caretaker had returned.
It had been struck to commemorate the silver jubilee of the
Grandson's accession.

Elias Khoury's Introduction

The Split Ego and the Hollows of Time

In London, where I now live disguised as an imaginary person, on the run from my mother's prophecy in which my original name rings as a terrifying memory ('Yahya, your soul will never know rest,' she said), it's hard to lie on the sloping tile roof of one's house and count the stars that have abandoned their positions.

With this passage Amjad Nasser ends the first poem in his latest collection, *Life as a Disrupted Narrative*. What's fascinating in this collection is how deeply he explores the lyricism of narrative, in that the poetry takes shape from the colourings of life, mixed with legend, and from the capacity of the moment to be so condensed that it becomes a compression of time.

The aim of this introduction is not to analyse a book of poetry that holds a special place on the map of contemporary Arabic poetry. But Amjad Nasser was mistaken when he believed that the best person to introduce his first novel to the reader would be a novelist, because the secret that no one believes when I reveal it is that what fascinates me in literature is the ability of words to compress time. Only poetry does that. That's why Scheherazade resorted to interlacing her magical stories with poetry, to reinforce the sense, as if the words of poetry are a nail we hammer into the wall of time. That's why novelists since Cervantes have turned narration into successive poetical moments, so that the story can absorb the pulse of things and their secret whispers.

When I reread *Life as a Disrupted Narrative*, I realised that it was only a matter of time before Amjad Nasser came to the novel, because the poet who has filled the gaps in time with poems must come round to writing time. And time is deceptive and slow, however rapid its capricious changes may be. We only have to reread his poem *A Young Woman in Costa Coffee* to discover that the story we will read in this book started there, when the young woman walked out of the poem and sat down in front of the poet to tell us about 'the poem that thought about another poem and then wrote it'.

When I began reading this book, I could smell the country that Amjad Nasser calls Hamiya. This smell has never left my skin since I went to Amman after the defeat of June 1967. The city is engraved in my memory by the term 'white city'. Memory is deceptive and, as we shall see in this novel, is a product of, or another name for, the imagination, or its image in the mirror of time. But Amjad Nasser is not telling the story of Jordan, but is using the fragrance of memory to write a delightful and profound novel about the hollows of time and the lessons of a life dissipated in exile.

In this novel the reader may find a story about Arab governments and also about the way they are opposed, and this is correct, because the whole eastern part of the Arab world has seen an illusion transformed into political and social facts that have become entrenched. I exclude Egypt here because its recent history is different, though it has now come to resemble other Hamiyas in almost everything.

This reading is not mistaken, and it may be a necessary one, as part of reading the transformations in Arab consciousness and to understand the major changes that have led to a conceptual upheaval at a time when fundamentalist currents are in the ascendant.

But I am not inclined to that reading. The magic of this text lies in its ambiguities and what is unspoken, and in the dualism with which the text glows, turning the narrative into a sturdy structure that reaches completion through what is missing and indulges in a nostalgia that avoids the temptation of nostalgia, but drinks the bitterness of nostalgia to the point of drunkenness.

In the beginning I believed I was dealing with something that resembled a memoir, only to discover that what looked like a memoir was only a trick. The novel uses the approach of a fictional autobiography, told in the first person, but the hero, a writer and a poet, splits in half: Younis and Adham. Younis is his real name; Adham is the pseudonym with which he signs his writings. This split, which seems at first sight to be the incarnation of the writer's real personality, rapidly vanishes when we discover other characters in the book and when we feel that the division of the ego is the structure of the novel, not its medium. The autobiographical approach has often been used in contemporary Arabic literature. Ghalib Halasa, who gave most of his heroes the name Ghalib, may have been the pioneer of this approach, but Amjad Nasser's novel and Halasa's story Sultana have something deeper in common than just this superficial approach. What unites them is the smell of place, the fragrance of memory that resists being dispersed by writing.

The narrative text begins at the first moment. Younis's, or Adham's, journey back to his homeland, after an absence of twenty years, forms the key to memory. We are dealing with a memory that reconstructs the past, not to recover it or mourn it, but as a mirror for the self. Younis stands in front of this mirror and finds someone else in front of him. And Roula is retrieved, not as an eternal love but as mother to the division that will afflict the narrator's son. Younis, who married on the Island of the Sun after the great exodus from the City of Siege and War, will name his son Badr, after the great Iraqi poet that he loves, and when he comes back to Hamiya he will discover that Roula has given her first son the same name, at a moment when the relationships and the significances are ambiguous, in that we don't know whether Younis is the father of the second Badr or whether the hero's division into two people will continue through two sons who bear the same name.

It's not conventional for an introduction to include literary criticism, but as I was reading and rereading this text, I found I couldn't stop talking about it. That stems from the magic of what I like to call the lyricism of the novel.

This lyricism has nothing to do with what we might call the lyrical novel, which pads the narrative text with meaningless poeticised meditations. It is the product of disciplined prose that is both economical and discursive, in order to tell the story. When the text succeeds in telling its stories, it restimulates the reader's appetite for the story, and in various forms. The lyricism of the novel opens the infinite doors of the story and takes us on a journey to a world where there are no longer any distinctions between reality and imagination, or between memory and dreaming.

The City of Nowhere that the reader comes upon through Amjad Nasser is the place where Arabic calligraphy intersects with poetry and with return to Noplace. In other words it's a literary place first and foremost and a framework in which we can see not only the treachery and helplessness of individuals, but also the treachery and vagaries of time, and the brutality of history.

The novel ends in the cemetery. Young Younis (the nephew of Younis al-Khattat) leads his uncle to the graveyard to visit the dead. The narrator doesn't tell us what he said to the dead nor what he heard from them. But this novel, like any great work of real literature, addresses the living in order to open a window for dialogue with the dead, making the hero's return to his country another journey into the unknown.

Elias Khoury

A NOTE ON THE AUTHOR

Amjad Nasser, a Jordanian poet born in 1955, has written numerous volumes of poetry and several travel memoirs. He has worked for newspapers in Beirut and Cyprus and since 1987 he has lived in London where he is managing editor and cultural editor of *Al-Quds Al-Arabi* daily newspaper. *Land of No Rain* is his first novel.

A NOTE ON THE TRANSLATOR

Jonathan Wright is a British journalist and literary translator, and the editor of the *Arab Media & Society* journal. He joined the Reuters news agency in 1980 as a correspondent, and has been based in the Middle East for most of the last three decades. His translations include *Taxi* by Khaled al-Khamissi and *Judgment Day* by Rasha al-Ameer.

A NOTE ON THE TYPE

The text of this book is set Adobe Garamond. It is one of several versions of Garamond based on the designs of Claude Garamond. It is thought that Garamond based his font on Bembo, cut in 1495 by Francesco Griffo in collaboration with the Italian printer Aldus Manutius. Garamond types were first used in books printed in Paris around 1532. Many of the present-day versions of this type are based on the *Typi Academiae* of Jean Jannon cut in Sedan in 1615.

Claude Garamond was born in Paris in 1480. He learned how to cut type from his father and by the age of fifteen he was able to fashion steel punches the size of a pica with great precision. At the age of sixty he was commissioned by King Francis I to design a Greek alphabet; for this he was given the honourable title of royal type founder. He died in 1561.